OUT OF THE FRYING PAN, INTO THE CHOIR

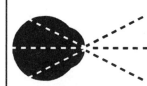

This Large Print Book carries the
Seal of Approval of N.A.V.H.

A RUBY, THE RABBI'S WIFE MYSTERY

OUT OF THE FRYING PAN, INTO THE CHOIR

SHARON KAHN

WHEELER PUBLISHING
An imprint of Thomson Gale, a part of The Thomson Corporation

Detroit • New York • San Francisco • New Haven, Conn. • Waterville, Maine • London

LIBRARY OF CONGRESS CATALOGING-IN-PUBLICATION DATA

Kahn, Sharon, 1934–
  Out of the frying pan, into the choir : a Ruby, the Rabbi's wife mystery /
by Sharon Kahn.
    p. cm. — (Wheeler Publishing large print softcover)
  ISBN-13: 978-1-59722-531-1 (lg. print : pbk. : alk. paper)
  ISBN-10: 1-59722-531-2 (lg. print : pbk. : alk. paper)
  1. Rothman, Ruby (Fictitious character) — Fiction. 2. Rabbis' spouses —
Fiction. 3. Jewish women — Fiction. 4. Choirs (Music) — Fiction. 5. Railroad
travel — Fiction. 6. Large type books. I. Title.
PS3561.A397O98 2007
813'.54—dc22   2007008104

Published in 2007 by arrangement with Scribner,
an imprint of Simon & Schuster, Inc.

Printed in the United States of America on permanent paper
10 9 8 7 6 5 4 3 2 1

*To my dear Camille,
who will be reading Ruby in the future.
May the stories you're writing continue
to bring the joy to you and to others that
they have to me.*

1

To the Favored Few
from Essie Sue (and Hal)
Annual Chanukah Letter

To all our family and selected friends:

It's potato latke time again! Time to consume (sparingly) those delicious holiday pancakes while reading my ever-popular review chronicling the achievements and accolades surrounding the Margolis clan. Be sure to lubricate your latkes with cooking spray until well done, top with a dollop of imitation sour cream (20 calories a tablespoon), add dietetic applesauce (counts as one fruit), and dig in.

Note: If you're on Atkins, fry up pure butter with Breakstone's sour cream into round mounds and skip the potatoes and the applesauce. Those celebrating both Christmas and Chanukah may optionally serve this dish over Atkins-approved fried pork rinds. Obviously, this does not include the rest of us.

Now for the news. People, this has been another outstanding year in the annals of our Margolis family history. In February, Essie Sue and Hal traveled to the exclusive Strait of Magellan with Hal's alumni group. Essie Sue was voted Voyager Most Suited for a Desert Island — quite an honor when one considers that she was disabled for three days after a regrettable encounter with the wildlife at mating season — namely, a female elephant seal who refused to be petted during her reproductive cycle. However, since the accident took place on an exclusive Added Expense Optional Trip, Essie Sue used the downtime to research Jews of the subantarctic forests. Unfortunately, there were none. (Unless, to be accurate, one counted both Margolises and Hal's two ZBT fraternity brothers, also on the tour.)

It is with great pleasure that Essie Sue and Hal announce the May graduation from Oxford of Essie Sue's grandnephew Phil. Since the graduate preferred to be in the company of family and friends for this Simchas, a facsimile was held in Oxford, Ohio, so that all could attend. Three cheers for Phil, and for his proud mother, Sara Lee, who wore a tiara for the occasion which bore the seal of the Royal Family.

In August, Essie Sue received the Woman of Value award from our town of Eternal's Chamber of Commerce, for her prolonged but successful effort to acquire three park benches from the county. Hindered for five years by County Commissioner Leroy (Bud) Gantry, Eternal finally secured the benches on the occasion of the commissioner's last living act from his bed in Memorial Hospital. As soon as the order was signed, Gantry received last rites from Father Terry Breen, a close friend of the Margolis family.

And last but not least, in November, Essie Sue was appointed head of Eternal fund-raising for the first Interdenominational ChoirFest in Lake Louise, Canada, in May. Our own choir at Temple Rita has been honored with an invitation to travel by train from Vancouver to Banff, and the tour will be financed by latke promotions to take place from December through April. Custom orders for latkes will make sales possible even after the Chanukah holiday, assuming continuing interest on the part of the public.

Essie Sue and Hal are indeed humbled by the well-deserved honors coming their way. They look forward to bigger and better accomplishments in the year ahead, and will rest assured knowing that you will all be eager to read about them in next year's Annual Chanukah Letter.

As it is written, "Our Cup Runneth Over. Surely goodness and mercy shall follow us all the days of our lives." Book of Psalms. Amended.

Happy Chanukah to all,
Essie Sue and Hal Margolis

2

Email to: Nan
From: Ruby
Subject: A lot on our plates besides
latkes

What's happening, girl? You left me in midsentence last night when we'd been on the phone for only five minutes. I'm assuming your cell phone conked out on you — surely you can do better in Seattle than the regional phone company you're using. I gave up after my third attempt to reconnect, and went to bed totally frustrated that I couldn't whine to you for at least an hour more.

I'm somewhat sorry I signed up for Essie Sue's trip to Canada, cheap as it is, because this means I have to help with the latke sales to finance it. I thought it was worthwhile because that train trip through the Canadian Rockies is supposed to be spectacular, but who knows if anything she sponsors is worth the aggravation? This comes at a good time, though, when I'm at loose ends.

Ed continues to haunt my dreams, even though it's over, over, over. It's getting better, though — I now spend only the first part of the night feeling wistful over the good bits, while the rest is taken up reliving the yucky parts. This is progress, I suppose, and I do know I did the right thing. The journalist in him overcame the human being just one time too many — and at least I'm not as miserable now that some time has passed.

I'm worried about *you,* though. Don't you think you need to get out of your doldrums and start mixing a little? Come down to Eternal and visit me if you can't find anyone in the big city. I'm advising a computer client in Austin I think you'd find attractive — he has hazel eyes, if you're interested.

Email to: Ruby
From: Nan
Subject: Green-eyed with envy

Yeah, I *am* mired in misery of my own making (no charge for the alliteration) but I'm getting tired of pushing myself, showing my best side, and pretending I'm having a great time with some guy when I'm not. I'm taking a vacation from that and have promised myself I can stay stuck for six more months before they cart me off.

BUT, you lucky dog, I don't see why you're whining at all . . . you might have ended it with Ed, but now you have Lieutenant Paul at your doorstep, don't you? And talk about sexy — he's definitely my type, even if he is a cop. Care to offer him up, or do I only get a crack at the computer client?

Email to: Nan
From: Ruby
Subject: RE Green-eyed with envy

Things are getting warmer with Paul, but I'm taking it easy. As for his being your type, you've known him for years, and he still praises you to the rafters for helping solve the bagel killing a few years ago. You're welcome to throw your hat (or in your case, barrister's wig) into the ring.

Email to: Ruby
From: Nan
Subject: Right

You're just saying that because you know you have the home-court advantage. I say go for it.

I'm taking some time off, even though I do have the hots for Paul. Which is why I shouldn't admit this, but you two do make an awfully cute couple with your matching green eyes and cat-swallowed-the-canary grins. I like the way your head just reaches to his shoulders, too.

And don't turn down that Canadian trip, either, Ruby — you never know.

3

"My podiatrist's sister-in-law Bitsy is a party planner, Rabbi. I think we should hire her to do the Chanukah latke event at temple. She's also a grief counselor."

Kevin Kapstein, the one and only rabbi in Eternal, Texas, looks at me for any cue as to how to respond to Essie Sue Margolis, lifetime chairwoman of the temple board. Essie Sue claims to revere his opinion as her spiritual leader, but also cosigns his contracts — a potent combination that usually paralyzes him into silence on these non-liturgical occasions.

Not me. "How much does she charge?" I ask.

"I wasn't talking to you, Ruby. I was telling the rabbi about someone who might be of service to us."

"Speaking of service," my partner Milt Aboud interrupts, "how many of you want cinnamon bagels with cream cheese, and how many choose sesame with lox?"

Milt owns the majority interest in The Hot Bagel, a venture I bought into several years ago after my husband and Kevin's predecessor, Rabbi Stu Rothman, was killed. While Milt runs the bakery, I keep our finances intact, a task made easier by my freelance work as a computer consultant for small businesses.

The six of us sitting at the round table by the window split evenly on the bagel choices — we should only be so accommodating on the subject at hand.

"You have to spend money to make money, Ruby," Essie Sue reminds me. "And the woman's a grief counselor, too. We'll be getting a twofer — it's a bargain."

"How much?" I ask again.

"Only two thousand dollars. And she'll throw in three sessions for any congregants who happen to be grieving during the time she's planning the party."

"But I thought I was the grief counselor," Kevin says in my ear. He's nervous about any preemptions, and understandably so.

"For less than that, I'll plan the party," I say.

"You're only an amateur, Ruby," Essie Sue says. "This woman is a professional. She planned for the sheriff's swearing-in cer-

17

emony before he was caught with the teen-ager. Tell Ruby how lovely that event would have been, Hal."

Hal Margolis, unlike his wife, is a man of few words, not all of them devoted to her support.

"You're asking me?" he says, sharing our common disbelief. "I think Ruby's right — the party planner's too expensive. Why don't you handle it? You'll end up telling her what to do anyway."

"Maybe you can get her to volunteer her services," I say. "After all, the congregational functions could be a gold mine for her once she's established. Maybe she'll do it for expenses."

"I'll work on her," Essie Sue says. I'm not sure if this instant agreement on her part is shock at Hal's independence or pure practicality, but we're going with it.

"All in favor of trying for a freebie, raise your hands," I say. It's unanimous, and that includes Rose Baker, the late Herman Geunther's daughter, who's looking great in one of her usual long skirts. She never adopted pants when the rest of us did. Rose has been a good friend of mine ever since we worked together to discover her father's killer a few years ago. She's the temple choir representative for this planning session, and

Essie Sue's already loaded her with responsibilities. I just hope we can help her.

"Rose, you're in charge of the program for the latke event," Essie Sue says. "The choir should recruit its best voices for our entertainment."

"The choir only has ten members, Essie Sue," Rose says, "and two of them don't sing, remember?"

"Don't sing?" Milt tries unsuccessfully to hide his snort. As the one serving the bagels and the only person present who's not a temple member, his self-appointed function at these meetings is to *ootz* Essie Sue.

"Keep your sarcasm to yourself, Milt," she says. "There's a good reason for it. Tell him, Rabbi."

"Essie Sue thinks it's more aesthetically balanced to have ten people than eight," he says. "And after Mel and Reneé Rafer moved away, we had two extra choir robes going to waste."

"I don't want to hear any more," Milt says, filling my cup with the mocha java he knows I love.

I give Milt a quick look over my shoulder as he pours. "You don't want to know what the two extras do?" I ask.

Kevin beats me to it. "They mouth the words. It's harder than it looks — I had to help them practice their Hebrew."

"It bulks up the presentation," Essie Sue says. "You'd be surprised how good it looks."

"I'm more concerned with how it sounds," Rose says, "but we'll take care of it. I'm enlisting the help of my good friend Serena to whip the program into shape. She's our top soprano, in my opinion. If you want our cooperation, just don't lean on us, Essie Sue."

"Your cooperation? This whole fund-raising event is for your benefit — it shouldn't cost you a penny to take this trip of a lifetime."

"I'll believe that when I see it," Rose says. "We haven't raised the money yet."

"I was going to use André Korman to be our driving influence for the choir," Essie Sue says, "not Serena Salit — she's such a health nut, whereas he's a forceful baritone."

"What's health got to do with leading the quartet?" Rose says. "I thought you said I was running the program, Essie Sue. If I am, then Serena's my choice, forceful or otherwise. And speaking of health nuts, André owns a health store — have you forgotten? He already thinks he's the choir director, which he's not, even though Serena seems to think he's something special. We all take turns directing, like the rabbi advised."

Sounds like Kevin's idea, although I've never heard of a choir without a director. André's forceful, all right — obnoxiously so, I'd say. I can't imagine his accepting any advice Kevin had to give. And I didn't know he was on Essie Sue's favorites list, either.

"So what are you envisioning?" I ask Rose. "A couple of songs?"

"Maybe more than that," she says. "Our best voices — Serena, André, Irene Cohn, and Serena's ex-husband Bart Goldman make up a quartet within the choir. They'll have to perform at least two selections, with the choir following up with a couple of others."

"That's not long enough," Essie Sue says. "We need a more complete program to entertain everyone."

"No." Rose and I react together, with Hal nodding his support.

"We'll put them to sleep with a long vocal program," Rose says. "Just let us take care of it, Essie Sue."

I suggest we adjourn the meeting before they come to blows. I should be so lucky.

"Hold on," Essie Sue says. "First we have to figure out how to get the carbohydrates out of the latkes. Rabbi, I'm appointing you to research this. Maybe the scholar Maimonides had something to say about it — I understand he was interested in weight loss."

"Huh? You mean from the fourteenth century?"

"Well, he *was* a doctor," Essie Sue says. "See if he was a cardiologist like the South Beach guy."

Kevin does what he usually does in these situations — he scribbles notes furiously. I shamelessly look under his bent arm to see what he's writing, but think better of it when I see that he's written the word *Google* over and over.

"Don't bother, Kevin," I whisper in his ear. "You know she forgets half the stuff she tells you to do."

"Easy for you to say, Ruby. I'm staying on her good side."

Well, I tried.

I get up to leave — definitely the only way to bring meetings with Essie Sue to an end — when she raises a magenta-taloned hand to my arm and pulls me back down.

"Ruby, I don't think you're seeing the selfish possibilities in this grief-counseling operation."

"Huh? I don't know from selfish, Essie Sue. Can you explain this in under two minutes?"

Since I can't begin to fathom how this woman's mind works, I usually find it best to give her a time limit for her revelations. I roll my eyes in Rose's direction for a reality check and notice that Rose is already biting her lip.

"I guess I'll have to spell it out for you," Essie Sue says. "You're a natural for Bitsy's first class."

"I still can't believe she calls herself *Bitsy*," Hal says. "That's a name for a grief counselor? A party planner, maybe."

"Not now, Hal. I'm telling Ruby about Bitsy's grief-counseling skills. Picture this, Ruby. You're sitting in the grief-counseling orientation session, trying to get over Stu's death."

"Whoa," I say. "He was killed years ago, and although I can't say I'll ever be over him, it's pretty clear I have moved on."

"So you need a little help, not a lot. But remember, Ruby, these sessions are coed. Some nice widower or divorced man — Bitsy does divorce grief, too — might have lost his loved one a short time ago. Before some pushy neighbor with a bowl of chicken soup can get her claws into him, you'll have the edge from the class. Look at the possibilities."

Rose chokes up her last swallow of coffee. "So you're saying we'll get a threefer, not a twofer?" she asks. "A grief counselor, a party planner, *and* a matchmaker?"

"See, Ruby — Rose gets it, and she's not even single. If you'd learned to be smart for yourself, you'd be married by now. You lost the journalist already, not that he was any great catch."

"Ruby's interested in someone else," Kevin says. "Lieutenant Paul Lundy — he always liked her."

"Do I look like I'm wearing Harry Potter's Cloak of Invisibility?" I ask as I stand up for a second time. "Lay off, everybody."

Milt tries to put his arm around me, a gesture I'd appreciate more if he wasn't cracking up at my expense.

Essie Sue's not finished, unfortunately. "Lundy the policeman? She'd be robbing the cradle, for starters."

"At least it's better than robbing the grave."

4

"Either your hair's gone curly or you've never let it grow long enough for me to tell," I say, reaching to tuck a dark lock of Paul's hair behind his ear. A very cute, nicely shaped ear, I might add — with a lobe that fits the tip of my thumb perfectly.

I'm relaxed just being out to dinner with him, not that the soothing Beefeater martini isn't doing its part.

"You're better now," he says, his smile still slightly dampened by concern. Paul's fussing over me tonight makes up for that dreadful lunch with my "good" friends treating me as though I weren't there.

"They were laughing at Essie Sue, not you," he reminds me.

"I know. I just get tired of being the feisty one who can hold her own no matter what," I say. "Sometimes I'm sick of all of it."

I like that Paul knows exactly when to squeeze my hand and when not to. We've been seated in one of those circular booths for four — it's all they had available. The good news is that we're side by side. The bad news is that we're talking side by side, too. I can't see him without turning.

"So you're robbing the cradle with me, huh?" Now his grin's back full force. "I had no idea five years made such a difference."

"She probably thinks you're younger," I say. "You look it."

"So do you. If you don't know that, you should. I'm glad you told me the whole story, though — lots of women wouldn't, if it emphasizes something they'd rather ignore. Like age."

"Yeah, well, that's me. I'd much prefer my own company to someone I can't be myself with. The added bonus with you is that I can trust you, too."

The waiter puts a piece of aromatic sea bass in front of me — I catch a whiff of ginger in the sauce.

"Couldn't you trust what Ed said?" Paul hides that zinger behind a twirling forkful of linguini.

I put my fork down and he does, too.

"Sorry," he says. "You didn't need that tonight."

"You're still hung up on Ed, aren't you?" I say. "Even now that I'm not."

"I guess I am," he says.

"What am I going to do about it?"

"You don't have to do anything, Ruby. It's my problem. It's just that when you brought up trust, I thought of Ed because that seemed to be a big sticking point with you — the fact that he might have been milking you to get background for his stories."

"That was a problem for me, but it's history. We broke up. Why go over it?"

"You were in love with him. If he hadn't had divided loyalties, maybe you'd still be with him. That was my observation, and I did a lot of observing."

"So you're saying if I hadn't had good reason to break up with Ed, we'd still be together, right? Pardon me if I say *duh* to that one, Paul. Isn't that why anyone ends a relationship? You're too smart for this kind of thinking."

He looks at me in a way that makes me want to backtrack. And I do.

"Okay, I know this has nothing to do with intelligence. It's what you feel. Are you worried that I'm not over him, or are you upset that we were together at all?"

"Both, I guess." He's not reaching for my hand this time, and he's calling for another martini.

"I can reassure you about the first," I say,

"but there's not much I can do about the second."

We eat in silence for a while. The sea bass no longer tastes as good.

"So where are we?" he says.

"Honestly, Paul?"

He nods, but not very convincingly. Still, it's enough of an opening to make me know I shouldn't finesse this.

"In answer to your question," I say, "I can't describe where we are. But I can tell you I'm not comfortable with where we are — does that make any sense?"

"Unfortunately, yes," he says. He instinctively offers me a sip of his martini, and I take it. I hate that he's still bothered by Ed. And I especially wish he wouldn't go into freeze mode whenever he's reminded of that relationship. I guess it's exacerbated because Paul's friendship with me was on the verge of taking a more serious turn just before Ed came along. There's nothing I can do about that interruption. I'm glad the affair is over, but I certainly don't regret it, either.

"Can't we give this some time, Paul?" I say as I try to enjoy the meal. "It'll work itself out."

"I guess I'm the one who needs to work some things out, Ruby."

"I can't argue with you there. Let's take a

deep breath, though, and not get so excited over this. Can we maybe talk about something else now?"

The neat part about Paul is that he's so often on my wavelength. Instead of pouting, he smiles at me. Granted, a sad smile, but he's trying, and so am I.

I have a ready-made icebreaker — I give him more details about Essie Sue's party planner and the upcoming latke event.

"Will it be an interminable evening?" he says.

"Is the rabbi Jewish? Of course it'll be long — Essie Sue's in charge of the preparations. Look at it as a test of your devotion."

"Not without some hope of payback," he says. "What's in it for me?"

"I'll owe you big," I say. "Who knows how you might collect?"

"You're wicked when you want something, Ruby."

"So you'll definitely come?"

"I promise I'll be there — I just don't know when. If things are busy, I know I can't get away as early as you might want. But look at it this way — since I'll be there for the last part of the evening, you'll be guaranteed a ride home."

"I'm driving," I say. "So I'll be guaranteed a police escort following me home — that's different. And are you sure you're not wimping out? If so, I'll have no choice but to set my sights on the first grieving widower I can find."

He answers me with a quick kiss, which I'd call delicate if he wasn't still chewing his linguini.

5

To say that our beloved Temple Rita is decked out for the evening would be an understatement. Canadian flags are all over the Blumberg Social Hall, signifying, I presume, the location of the ChoirFest in Lake Louise. Bitsy, the party planner, was apparently at a loss to think of other decorations that might remind us of our neighbor to the north, but she did come up with snow. Lots of snow — the artificial kind, of course.

"Bitsy lucked out," Essie Sue tells me. "Since it's the Christmas season, too, she was able to grab all the snowflakes from the hobby store before the church groups got to them. Now *that's* creative."

"No, that's cruisin' for a bruisin'," I say.

Bitsy herself materializes from a cloud of white — it's my first glimpse of her. Her administrative style is of the distant variety — she's directed this production by telephone and email as much as possible. Maybe she's smarter than I thought to avoid clashing with Essie Sue in full party mode.

"You're only seeing Bitsy in her planner role, Ruby," Essie Sue says as she throws one of her welcoming headlocks on an unsuspecting Bitsy and draws her close. "I want you to get to know her grief personality, too. This could be to your benefit."

Although Bitsy relaxes as Essie Sue loosens her grip, this is obviously not a woman who lets go easily. Definitely a type A, Bitsy looks more party planner than grief counselor. Tall and blond, she's got to be pushing fifty, but you're not meant to guess it from the ring in her navel, Alice in Wonderland locks to her shoulders, and baby-doll eyes with more blue on the lids than in the iris.

"She's very fashionable with the emphasis on the midriff," Essie Sue faux-whispers to me. I find myself more fascinated with the metal than the midriff — the ring looks tarnished, and I'm sure that's a no-no, hygiene-wise.

I try really hard to pull my eyes away, but don't quite make it.

"Admiring my ring?" Bitsy says. "I can give you the name of the guy who put it in if you want."

"Not this year," I say, unhappy that I have

no one nearby to roll my eyes at. "My trainer at the gym made me swear off round objects attached to my organs — I have to stay clean until the scars heal."

"Oh." Bitsy seems unfazed by my revelations, and Essie Sue never listens anyway. She's already switching gears.

"I have to make a surprise announcement," she says, grabbing the nearest glass to tap on. She does it carefully with the insides of her first two fingernails.

"Ladies and gentlemen — I want to report that through some tough negotiations and great generosity, our party planner has produced and directed this event for fifteen hundred dollars less than she charges her real clients. She expects you to repay her by booking her for your own celebrations. Bitsy is available for the usual bar and bat mitzvahs, weddings, and anniversaries. I want a big round of applause before we proceed to the next part of our program."

What a tribute. Even though it's obvious that Bitsy's downsized and cut a few corners, the event is still supposedly a bargain. Aside from the hobby-shop cheapo snowflakes, we've been treated so far to Canadian Iced Decaf, Frozen Tundra Chanukah Latkes (definitely frozen), and multicolor Kool Pops representing nothing that I can see, although I'm sure she had something in mind.

Essie Sue's also insisted on no-fat sour cream to top the potato latkes, which, to my mind, is like making love without sex. And if these are the latkes we're depending on to make money for the trip, we're in deep doo-doo. Not that anyone's eaten enough to get sick — I was pressed into service at the buffet table, and we had orders to serve each person only two thin pancakes.

While Bitsy's talking to a prospective client, I pull on Essie Sue's arm.

"Bitsy who?" I ask. "You forgot to properly introduce her."

"I already did, Ruby."

"What's her name, then?"

"Bitsy."

"That's it?"

"As in *Cher*. And *Barbra*. And *Madonna*."

"Do you like that, Ruby? My stand-alone name?"

Bitsy's back. I hope she's not gonna tell me the name of a guy who can get me one.

"Sure," I say, "I like it if you do."

"It looks great on my business cards, and it leaves room for the logos."

I take the card she hands me. I should have guessed — a happy face and a sad face flanking the stand-alone *Bitsy*.

"I dropped my last name when I dropped my last husband," she says. "It's simpler."

I can't argue with her logic, just her logos. But hey, she's giving us this two-thousand-dollar affair for a mere five hundred dollars, even though she's still making a hundred percent profit, from the looks of things. I'd say this party cost about two fifty.

"Hey, Essie Sue, the choir is ready. When do they go on?" Kevin yells from behind a curtain onstage — his subtle signal that the program is about to begin. I'm relieved to get away from both Essie Sue and the redoubtable Bitsy, and I look around for Rose, who's running the show. I hope. Of course, no show really runs around here without Essie Sue's okay.

"Tell Rose she can start," Essie Sue says.

With a big fanfare from Mr. Wolkin, our new organist, who's at the social hall piano, the curtain opens. The Temple Rita choir, robed in blue, with white cardboard collars in the shape of, right — snowflakes, a Bitsy touch, I'm sure — takes a deep bow. All twelve choir members, including the two fillers, join in the first two songs — rehashed versions from Friday-night services. I'm seriously worried that with these for openers, the crowd won't hold — especially since the Kool Pops seem to have been the last of the refreshments. Make that 150 bucks that Bitsy spent on this extravaganza.

I glimpse Rose directing traffic backstage as the full choir leaves, and run back to check in with her.

"I know," she says. "Don't even tell me — those first two songs weren't even on the list — Essie Sue threw a fit and insisted that we lengthen the program, and the only other songs the group felt comfortable singing were the ones you just heard. I should have put them at the end."

"I know what you're working with," I say, "it's just that I'm afraid it's getting *too* comfortable out there, if you know what I mean."

"It should perk up a little," she says. "I've changed the order and put the quartet in right now."

The four members of the quartet step to the front of the stage, and I plunk myself in the front row beside Kevin.

Serena Salit's my favorite, although most of what I know of her is through Rose. She was married for years to Bart Goldman, baritone in our quartet, and they divorced a year ago. Bart's a doctor — a nice guy but a little uptight. Serena's got a great sense of humor — at least about everything except her vitamin fetish. Rose says she could open

36

her own health food store, so I'm sure she's given André lots of business since he moved here. I think her divorce was pretty stressful, but aren't they all? She and Bart have managed to stay in the choir together despite the split.

The tenor is André Korman. He and his wife, Sara, are relative newcomers — they've been in town three or four years now. I seem to remember that Sara's family is fairly well to do, and once had some dealings with Hal Margolis, which is probably why they're on Essie Sue's favorites list. I can take Sara, but André's so full of himself. I heard *André* used to be *Arnie* before he changed it.

He looks like the Dapper Dan in a Chaplain movie — sporty little mustache, immaculate shirt collars that look as though they're starched, a year-round tan, and a gold ring on each hand. Even though he owns Eternal's health food store, they live way beyond what that could support — courtesy of the wife's side, I guess.

Irene Cohen, our alto, is part of an old Eternal family — she's a violinist as well as a singer. She's quite attractive, and I know of at least two guys she's gone with — don't know who her current boyfriend is. André seems to have an eye for her, but then, that's his persona — he considers himself irresist-ible.

Serena Salit signals to the accompanist to begin the introductory passage, but André shakes his head. He leans over to the micro-phone and says, "Sorry, all, we'll start in a moment." Great, they haven't sung a note, and already he's pulling a power play. I glimpse Rose fuming in the wings.

To no one's great surprise, Serena caves. I feel for her — she's probably trying to avoid a scene in front of all these people. André takes over and the song begins. They're try-ing something from *Yentl,* which André's arranged for four voices — you can bet without permission from Barbra. Since the piece was written as a solo, it took quite a bit of arranging, none of it successful. Rose peers at me from the wings and shrugs, but before the audience can react one way or the other, Essie Sue jumps up onstage and leads the applause — or should I say, demands it.

Like so many wonders she initiates, it works, and the audience is actually clap-ping, if in a backhanded sort of way.

I'm beginning to hope they only have two songs for us — this applause on demand can go on only for so long. Essie Sue herself signals the pianist to begin the next selection — a move which even André doesn't dare question. This one's a Yiddish folk song, and they're doing it as a round. Bart Goldman's baritone is crisp and assured — a good start. Irene's next, and sails through the alto part. I see a relieved grin on Rose's face backstage, and I'm almost relaxed enough to go into daydreaming mode, when the sound of silence intervenes. Instead of Serena's soprano, I hear, well, nothing.

I rouse myself fast and refocus my eyes on the stage. Serena's standing there, looking as if singing *should* be coming from her open mouth, but it's not. She seems normal enough, as though she's preparing to get a sound out. It's like a mime has taken over, using gestures instead of words.

Suddenly, normality vanishes and she struggles. Both hands flutter around her chest, and then she clutches harder. She sinks straight down toward the stage floor, her legs giving way under her until she's briefly sitting, then crumpling at the waist and folding over, her arms stretched to one side, like a ballerina taking a bow.

6

It's difficult to focus on the chaos in front of me, and my eyes go straight to Rose, standing backstage. She sees me, too. Her jaw drops and she's frozen for a moment, just before she rushes forward to join what's now a jumble of forms and sounds:

"Get over to her."

"No, stay away, let her have air."

"Looks like she's had a heart attack."

"No, she's just fainted."

Irene and Bart are bending over Serena, and André's pulling them off.

"Unless you're going to give her artificial respiration," he says, "give her some room."

"They say you're not supposed to do that anymore — it can be harmful to the patient," Essie Sue says from the front row. "Don't touch her until we get a doctor."

She turns to the audience. "Is there a physician in the house?"

"Bart's a doctor, Essie Sue — you know

that," someone yells from the back of the room.

Bart's already on the case, and is the only one with the presence of mind to grab his cell. As he calls with one hand, he kneels and touches Serena's neck with the other — I guess he's feeling for a pulse.

I stay put — there are enough people up there as it is. As far as I can tell, Serena's not moving.

Kevin turns and looks at me. His face is pale and miserable — his usual countenance during emergencies like this, when he's wishing he could be anyplace else.

"This isn't the time I'm supposed to do something, is it, Ruby? I mean, this is a medical situation, right? Unless you think I should be counseling the choir members."

"I'd stay put if I were you, Kevin. Let's just hope your services won't be needed."

Essie Sue edges toward me. "Ruby, how long do you think it will take for Bart to get a stretcher here?" she whispers from the side of her mouth.

"I don't know. Sometimes it seems to take ages. Do you think they won't make it in time?"

"That, too, but the audience needs direction. We won't be able to keep them if nothing's happening onstage. And I haven't passed the sign-up sheets for the frozen latke sales. This whole urgent event was to raise their consciousness."

"Well, at the moment we're raising their blood pressure," I say. "They're adults — they don't need direction to see what's happening. There are some situations you can't control, Essie Sue, and this is one of them. You can at least wait until they take her to the hospital."

"The program?"

"It's over. Do a mailing about the latke sales."

"No way! That costs a fortune."

"Then go consult your grief planner," I say. "I can only deal with one thing at a time, and I'm concerned about Serena, as you should be."

"You're a lifesaver, Ruby. Bitsy's the perfect choice."

Fortunately for Kevin, Essie Sue seems to have forgotten about him. He's shrunk down in his chair to ensure things stay that way. I'm headed over to get a better view of the stage and maybe speak to Bart, when I hear Essie Sue tinkling on a glass. Actually, she's not tinkling, she's banging on it, and I'm expecting a shatter of shards any minute now. Bitsy's in tow, looking slightly shell-shocked.

"More help will come soon, ladies and gentlemen," Essie Sue says. "Meanwhile, remain in your seats while Bitsy passes out the sign-up sheet we've prepared for volunteer latke salespeople."

She couldn't have thought of a faster way to empty the house if she'd arranged it. As if on cue, everyone makes for the exits, most of them remaining outside to wait for the ambulance. Only a few die-hards choose to wait inside on pain of being accosted by our new party planner.

Bitsy, caught between looking cheerily upbeat to encourage signatures, and appropriately downcast to reflect current circumstances, is no doubt wishing she'd never volunteered, either. I just hope the grief part of her job won't materialize concurrently with the party part, and that Serena gets to the hospital fast.

I'm wondering whether it even makes sense to approach Rose while she's keeping her vigil beside Serena, when I hear a buzzing among the few audience members in their seats.

"Why are the police here?" I hear someone say.

I look around, see Paul in the back of the room, and wave him over. Since he's in a suit, and drives an unmarked car, I'm

43

wondering how the busybodies identified him, but then remember that this is a small town. Plus, he's had plenty of experience with Temple Rita, unfortunately.

"What's up?" he says in a low voice as he comes over to me.

"Why did the police get called?" I say, realizing I've just echoed everyone else.

"You're not surprised to see me, are you, hon?" he says. "You invited me, remember?"

"I did forget," I say, pointing toward the stage. "We've got an emergency here. Serena, one of our singers —"

"She's down?"

Paul takes off like a jaguar and springs onstage with that lithe grace that always amazes me when he's working. I hear André ask if he's another doctor, and some of the choir members look alarmed and a bit confused when he says he's police.

"You're here to help?" Bart says. "I'm her ex-husband."

I see Paul crouch down and use his cell while he looks at Serena — maybe he can get faster action than Bart did. Before he can do anything else, though, the EMT people arrive, thank goodness.

Two guys come in, lay down a stretcher right onstage, and start doing their thing, under Bart's direction. I see Paul talking to

44

the one taking Serena's pulse while the other unwinds some equipment, and then Paul helps clear the area. He blocks our view, deliberately, I'm sure, and asks those onstage to step down. I'm anxious to talk to Rose, who comes and sits by me.

"Can I get you some water or coffee?" I say, putting my arm around her.

She shakes her head no. "She's just so . . . so quiet," she says. "I know she was in pain because I saw her grab her chest, but it all happened so fast she never even cried out. Now she won't respond at all."

"Maybe she's in shock," I say. "Is there someone else we should call to meet her at the hospital?"

"Aside from Bart, she has no family here. She and Bart are on speaking terms, but I wouldn't exactly call them friends now, but he's a good doctor, thank heavens. I can't think of anyone else who's a relation. She has a sister in Ohio she's very close to, though."

"Okay, then I guess everything's covered."

"Will you go to the hospital with me?" Rose says. She seems shaky. "I've called home and told Ray and Jackie to go to bed if I'm out late."

"I don't think you need to be driving," I say. "I'll take you, and we can pick up your car after we go to the hospital. Maybe Paul will take both of us."

Paul and I had been hoping to spend a little time together tonight, but that's not going to happen. I know he'll be glad to take us over. Now that I think of it, though, he might not want to hang out at the hospital, so maybe I'd better drive my own car.

I talk Rose into having a little tea, and wait for Paul to do his work with the medics.

"What happened to the choir?" I say. "I don't see many of them up there."

The place has emptied out fast — I don't even see the other members of the quartet, except for Bart. Now more people are outside than in.

"Bart told us we should go home and check on Serena later when she gets to the hospital," Rose said.

"Rose, do you feel comfortable being around Serena when Bart's here?" I ask.

"You and your instincts, Ruby. No, frankly I don't. I just heard too much during the divorce trauma for me to be friendly with Bart. But in an emergency, I guess the rules don't apply. I'm definitely staying with her, though."

"You'd think the rest of the quartet would

be here at the very least," I say, "not to mention the choir."

"Until a few minutes ago I couldn't keep them all out of her face," Rose says. "Now I don't know where they are. It's probably for the best, though, that the crowd has cleared."

I see some stirring among the medics, and wonder if that's a good or bad sign.

It appears to be a good one. Paul comes down from the stage and puts his arms around the two of us.

"They found a pulse," he says.

7

As Rose and I walk down the hospital corridor to get some coffee, I'm sorry Paul and I had no time to talk. Not that he wouldn't have come with us, but I knew it would be pointless for him to stay, so I discouraged him, saying I'd call when I heard something. Paul had only showed up at temple because I'd invited him, and he'd never laid eyes on Serena until tonight. I don't know her that well myself, but if I can help Rose by being here, I will.

The crowd at temple may have diminished, but here at the hospital, Serena's friends seem to have multiplied. Essie Sue and Hal are here, plus Kevin, and two or three choir members. Serena's internist is here, and Bart's conferring with him. Hal's tired and is trying to persuade Essie Sue to go home, but she's undoubtedly afraid she'll miss something.

"They're sure taking a lot of time," Rose

says as we walk away from the group.

"Maybe you should call Serena's sister," I say.

"My gut tells me to wait at least until her internist comes out," Rose says. "I need to have *something* concrete to tell the woman. Unless you think I'm just procrastinating because I don't want to be the bearer of bad news."

"No, you're probably right, and a few minutes aren't going to make any difference — it's not as if she lives here in town and can rush right over."

Rose pours something molasses-like into two Styrofoam cups. "I think this is supposed to be coffee," she says. We both stare into our cups, waiting for the other to taste first.

"Bart had Serena's sister's number in his Palm Pilot," Rose says. "The sister's name is Joellyn Frank, and she lives in Cincinnati. She's married with a couple of kids, I think. Serena and Bart didn't have any children."

"So why do you think Serena and Bart stayed in the quartet together after the divorce?" I ask as we head back to the waiting room.

"Frankly? Pure stubbornness, I suspect. They both liked to sing, and neither of them was about to be pushed out of the quartet by the other. And who knows — maybe it showed that they were still tied to one another in some weird way. Maybe, given enough time, they might have gotten back together. I doubt it, but stranger things have happened."

"Where were you for so long?" Essie Sue says to me as we join the others. "I was about to send the rabbi after you."

"Any word?" I say.

"None," Kevin says. He looks upset, and knowing Kevin, it's probably not just about Serena.

"Don't worry," I lean over and say to him, "you're not supposed to be doing anything. Just relax."

"Did anyone notice something unusual just before she keeled over?" Essie Sue asks.

She draws blanks from all of us.

"Was she healthy, Rose?"

"Nothing wrong with her at all," Rose says.

This is making me nervous, and I'm about to go find the water fountain when the doctor comes out.

Rose stands up. "How is she?" she says.

"We lost her," he says, taking Rose's hand. "I'm very sorry."

We're stunned. I think we all assumed that when the EMT people found her pulse and started working on her back at the temple, she was, well, not out of danger, but definitely in the land of the living.

Rose sits down with the rest of us, and nobody says anything.

Her doctor seems uncomfortable with the silence. "Is there anything you want to ask?" he says. "Is there a next of kin present besides Dr. Goldman?"

We all look at each other, and then shake our heads no.

"I guess I'm actually the closest in town," Bart says. "We've been divorced about a year."

Rose is crying and clearly in shock, so I try to take her place. I tell the doctor about Serena's sister in Ohio and then ask what we're all wondering.

"What happened to her?" I say.

"Cardiac arrest — her heart stopped again when they were taking her out of the ambulance. When we put her on the table in the emergency room, we hoped to get her started again, but nothing worked. We were too late."

"She never even saw you, except for annual checkups," Bart says to the other doctor. "At least while we were married." He's trying to keep it together, but I can see his hand shake.

"We should have had her flown to Houston instead of to the hospital," Essie Sue says. "They can work miracles with heart transplants."

This is the doctor's cue to give us his card for later review and excuse himself for other emergencies — smart man.

Bart, who's held up until now, suddenly folds and says he wants to go home.

"Maybe the rabbi can take care of the preparations," he says.

Now I *know* he's not thinking clearly. Since Rose appears to be in no condition to do anything, and I wouldn't trust Essie Sue to impart bad news to anyone, I attempt to clear the room. I ask Hal to persuade Essie Sue to go home, ask Kevin and Rose to stay for a bit, and ease everyone else back to their cars.

Rose's functioning doesn't improve when the others leave.

"Ruby," she says, "could you make the arrangements here? And if I give you the number, would you call Joellyn in Cincinnati? Maybe Rabbi Kapstein could drive me home — I need to be with my family."

"Sure," I say.

"I'm sorry. I know I shouldn't fink out like this, for Serena's sake."

Kevin seems glad to have something to do

that doesn't involve making arrangements, and although he might be helpful later, I send him along with Rose.

When they've all gone, a nurse comes out and asks if I'm in charge of the deceased.

Apparently, I am. I was fairly effective during these moments when I was a rabbi's wife, but since Stu was killed, I don't do death well at all. Too many memories, too many churning emotions.

There are only two other people here — a mother with a crying baby and a man with what appears to be a sprained ankle. I wish Bart had stayed, but maybe the fact that he's an ex complicates things for him.

I want to go in and see Serena, and I need to call her sister.

I do neither. I just wait. This is a waiting room, and I wait.

Finally, I ask to look at her. Serena's lying peacefully on the gurney, tubes removed, her longish brown hair spread out on the pillow and her face turned to one side. I take her hand and hold it. It's still warm.

A loved one should be here for you, I think.

And for me. I most definitely need a loved one.

A few minutes pass, and as if in answer to my thoughts, Paul walks through the door

I've left ajar.

"You didn't call," he says quietly. "I thought of phoning, but I decided to come over."

I can't say anything back right now, but he doesn't seem to expect it. We stand by Serena for quite a long time, his arm around my waist and mine around his.

8

The Temple Rita sanctuary is strangely silent this afternoon as we wait for Serena's memorial tribute to begin. It's so quiet in here you can hear a prayer book drop — emphasizing for me once again the contrast between sudden death and any other. Our congregants are not exactly known for their decorum — there's always a buzz in the temple before a service, even a funeral service. Last week when ninety-year-old Harry Bloch was laid to rest, the rabbi had to shush the crowd twice just to be heard.

Granted, Kevin's not at his best on these occasions, and today is no exception. He's having trouble herding the choir onto the platform along with the temple executive board. Essie Sue's insisted that they all take part in the ceremony. Since Serena's family is out of town and planning to have their own burial service when the body is flown to Ohio, Essie Sue has no opposition —

certainly not from Kevin.

I'm sitting with Rose and her family while Kevin begins a lumbering attempt to introduce all those on the program.

"How long is he going to take, Ruby?" Rose asks me. She was supposed to sing with the choir, but wasn't up to it. I don't blame her — of all the people here, she was closest to Serena, and she's taking her death hard.

"I like the old-style funerals," she whispers, "where the mourners could grieve in silence while the rabbi took charge of the service and gave the eulogy. Now everyone has to get their two cents in, you know? I've even seen people that the deceased couldn't stand get up there and intone as if they were best friends."

"I have to admit this has aspects of a city council meeting," I say, "although I like hearing mourners speak when they have something to say and can do it with some taste. Just relax and think your own thoughts — that's what I'm doing." I don't add that going into my head is my chief coping strategy with *anything* that happens at the temple these days. And that anything is better than Kevin's eulogies.

After the choir has performed too many numbers and the board members have made their speeches, the three remaining members of Serena's quartet take their turns.

André Korman goes first. Although he seems genuinely moved by Serena's death — his hands are shaking a bit as he holds his notes — what he has to say seems vaguely out of key with the occasion. The subject is Serena, but it's all about him. He drones on about how he solicited her for the choir, how he needed a specific combination of voices and she completed the blend, and how she always answered the call of duty when he commanded. Kind of like an Essie Sue in male clothing. He makes a big deal about how he and his wife were so close to Serena.

Rose is rolling her eyes. "Serena never even mentioned André's wife to me," she says. "She never shows up at anything."

"Yeah, I know her," I say. I'm happy to see that Rose's husband, Ray, who's sitting on the other side of her, has grabbed her hand for support. I can see how difficult this is for her.

André ends by saying that "Serena, under my guidance, was beginning to understand what lies beneath the layers of our Jewish lives."

That one gets a collective eyebrow lift

from the congregation, not to mention our little group in the first row.

If André's remarks are odd, those of the next speaker, Irene Cohn, are even more so. She continues where André left off. After delivering the requisite litany of Serena's virtues of dedication and diligence — none of which reveals in the slightest what kind of person she was — Irene tells us that "Serena Salit was a promising initiate into depths unknown to ordinary plodders."

"Huh?" I say, nudging Rose. "Did I miss something?"

André is either congratulating Irene on her presentation or conferring with her — I can't tell which. She makes a couple of bland concluding remarks and sits down. I see Kevin looking at his watch. He's probably wondering if he can skip his eulogy, considering the length of the program so far.

The third quartet member, Serena's ex-husband, Bart Goldman, gets up and spends most of his allotted time on how uncomfortable he is in speaking about Serena when they've been divorced for so little time.

"This is a fiasco," Rose says. "The rabbi ought to do something about it."

That'll be the day. Mercifully, though, Essie Sue takes over, apparently deciding that the eulogizing needs to end. I see Kevin eagerly nodding his head at that — he's off the hook. For a change, even *I'm* glad she's taking charge.

"People," she says, "thus endeth the life of Serena Salit. The rabbi tells me that there will be no continuation of the service at the cemetery since the deceased will be buried at another ceremony in Ohio at the home of her sister."

Kevin stands up, apparently feeling the need to say *something* in clarification. Big mistake.

"I think Essie Sue means buried at the *cemetery* of her sister, not her home," he says. "Or maybe the cemetery in her sister's hometown." He looks to Essie Sue for confirmation, but doesn't receive it, now that he's not only corrected her in public, but also put the final stamp of confusion on a most forgettable day. Serena deserved better.

9

Email to: Nan
From: Ruby
Subject: Stuff

No, I'm actually not that excited about the choir trip yet — Serena's death has us all reeling here. I knew you'd be nauseous over the funeral details at the temple. I hear through the grapevine that the service and burial in Ohio went well (or as well as a funeral can) — she had lots of friends there.

Paul was beyond wonderful through all this, Nan — he becomes more endearing each time I see him. It's not just that he seems to know who I really am — he also supports me in a way no one has since my marriage. But I have a horror of falling too far too fast, when I'm barely over the fiasco with Ed. I know Paul senses this, too . . . hell, he doesn't just sense it, he's usually fixated on it. Which is one of our problems.

Email to: Ruby
From: Nan
Subject: Relax

Ha . . . I guess you're laughing at my telling you to relax when I'm usually advising you to get a grip, but this time I think you need to enjoy some of what's going on in your life. Do you realize that people wait years to find someone like this guy? Okay, I know I'm pushing, but at least don't take him for granted.

And I do get it about the trip. Another thing . . . although the scenery in the Canadian Rockies is fabulous, the idea that this is a choir trip is a bit dreary, isn't it?

Email to: Nan
From: Ruby
Subject: Trip

Yes and no. I know what you mean by *dull,* but this might not be. I've told you about the new emphasis on the Kabbalah and some of the more expressive elements in Judaism these days. True, you got as excited about it as I thought you might, knowing your preference for the rational, but since I'm always open to new stuff on the Jewish horizon, I'd like to see what's out there. And what's out there is definitely nothing Kevin knows about or will ever bring to our little outpost in Eternal. Some of the people exploring this sort of thing will be at this choir conference. Music's a big part of it, and who knows — I might learn something.

Email to: Ruby
From: Nan
Subject: Pu-leese

Remember that old song, Ruby — "Accentuate the positive, eliminate the negative, and don't mess with Mr. In Between"? I don't want to hear that you, of all people, are going Woo Woo on me. It doesn't suit you.

Email to: Nan
From: Ruby
Subject: Woo Woo

It's just a point of interest, babe.

Email to: Ruby
From: Nan
Subject: RE Woo Woo

Yeah. I've heard *that* before.

Email to: Nan
From: Ruby
Subject: P.S.

Forgot to tell you I think Kevin has a crush on Bitsy, the new grief counselor. This can only come to grief (you'll pardon the expression).

10

Kevin's car wouldn't start, so I'm picking him up tonight for Essie Sue's emergency meeting at Temple Rita. I'm looking forward to it, for a change, since it'll give me a chance to pump him about his new love interest. First, though, we have to make a stop at the vet's. She's working evening hours tonight and is giving my own personal adoring couple their shots while I'm at temple.

Oy Vey, my three-legged retriever, gives a low growl as Kevin backs his way into the front seat. She's usually placid, but she's never taken to Kevin.

"Why's she in the cage?" he asks, adding, "Not that I'm unhappy about it."

"I admit you're not on her top-ten list, but she certainly wouldn't hurt you, Kevin. I used her old crate to transport Chutzpah, the cat I was keeping for Joshie. When Oy Vey saw Chutzpah in the dog carrier, she crawled in after him and wouldn't get out."

"Aren't they supposed to hate one another? As in 'fighting like cats and dogs'? I'm not a pet person, but even I know that."

"They're in love. As in 'wild about each other.' Chutzpah even sleeps on Oy Vey's back at night. When Joshie brought the cat home on his last visit, I thought for a while that they'd be enemies, but they've done a complete turnaround. Now I can't separate them."

"So you're keeping him? I thought Josh was just bringing him home to Momma temporarily because he didn't have room for him in his girlfriend's apartment."

"It's permanent now — they're a pair. And speaking of couples, what's up with you and little miss one-name? I hear you have the hots for Bitsy. Planning any private parties?"

Kevin doesn't blush — he does the reverse. His face loses all color when he's teased.

"Quit it, Ruby — she's just a friend."

"I've heard that before, and said it a few times, too."

"But it's true. We haven't even had a date."

"Well, if you ask me, the party planning and grief counseling would look pretty good

66

on her *rebbetzin* résumé."

"They didn't look so good on yours."

"Touché. You're getting a lot looser these days, Kevin."

"That's because I know you're not out to get me, Ruby."

"Come on, you've got to drop some of that paranoia. If Stu and I hadn't developed a thick skin early on, we'd have been long gone. You have to give it back to them in kind when people start pressuring you."

"Easy for you to say — you're not doing this job anymore. I have to watch my every move." He's biting his nails again, but I try not to notice.

"Then it's even more important to have some fun on your off hours. Who started this flirtation, you or Bitsy? As if I have to ask."

"I guess she did. She called and asked me out."

"And you said no to a date?"

"Well, I said I'd think about it. She wanted to know how many days I had to have before I accepted."

"Just the kind of girl you need, Kevin."

"You mean you're encouraging this? I thought you said she was trivial."

"Trivial's good at this stage. What do you have to lose? Bitsy's even cute, in a . . ."

"Trivial sort of way?"

"Maybe she'll be able to get you out of those black wing-tipped shoes and into something more twenty-first century. Somebody needs to grab you, boy. You're already way smarter than she is." I reach over and pat his knee. Bad idea.

"How about you?" he says.

"We've covered this territory before, Kevin. After all these years, I feel closer to you than I ever thought I would, but this is not a romance. Remember when I went to that temple dance with you and you told everyone we were dating? I'm not going through that again."

Fortunately, we're pulling up to the vet's and I'm off the hook until the next time.

I open the door to the crate and we have to bribe Oy Vey with a dog cookie to get him out. Chutzpah immediately goes into a shrill whine, which doesn't let up the whole time we're at the front desk. The vet promises me she'll keep them together for the staff's sake as well as for theirs.

Bitsy's car pulls up to the temple just as we do, and Kevin's face loses color again. She gets out to walk in with us, doing a kissy kissy in the air by my cheek, and giving him a real one on the lips. A quick one, though — she obviously doesn't want him to freak in front of me.

"So how are you?" she says to him, twirling his index finger while she gazes at him. "I didn't know you and Ruby were good friends."

Kevin and I look at each other — this is one of those questions with no answer, under the circumstances. We don't want to say we are, and we don't want to say we aren't. It didn't even occur to me until now that she might consider me, of all people, a rival.

"We're old friends," I say, "sometimes good, sometimes not so good, huh, Kevin?"

Not a great line on my part, and it leaves him looking utterly bewildered as to how to reply.

"I guess so," he says finally. "Aren't we late?"

We *are* late, so we avoid further awkwardness and head inside, where we're ushered to the front row of a darkened Blumberg Social Hall.

"I saved you seats," Essie Sue says, interrupting her slide presentation and turning on the lights. "I need you on the front row. Why are you late, Rabbi?"

"It was Ruby's fault," Kevin says.

This, in essence, is why our relationship will forever remain at arm's length. The boundaries of Kevin's support extend only as far as his narcissism will permit. To put it even more bluntly, he'll drop me faster than a hot latke to save his own skin.

"Ruby had to go to the vet with the dog and cat," he says. "If I'd thought we would be late, I'd have stopped her."

"You should have reminded her this is why Jews and animals don't mix," Essie Sue announces. "And as I've told you many times, Ruby, wild creatures in rabbinical families are especially ludicrous. It's like making a ham sandwich on challah bread."

"Unfortunately for you, Essie Sue, I'm not in a rabbinical family anymore, and if you don't get off my back in sixty seconds, I'll illustrate that."

The lights go down in ten, and we're treated to a history of the latke, illuminated with hand drawings by Essie Sue's niece Sherry, age six.

"Chanukah's over," Kevin faux-whispers to me. "Why does she think we can take fund-raising orders for these in January?"

Apparently, he doesn't realize I'm not speaking to him after the blame game I just witnessed. I close my eyes and hope for a few more minutes of blessed darkness before some sort of surreal discussion begins.

I don't have long to wait.

"Have I put you all in the mood now? Are you latke-motivated?"

Essie Sue turns off the projector and points to Bitsy, her newly appointed shill, who jumps up and raises both fists in the air with a *yay*. I think that's supposed to rouse us, but it's about as effective as the Dallas cheerleaders are when the Cowboys are losing. And a lot less sexy.

Not that this daunts Essie Sue.

"I want to tell you about something that's just come into my life, people," she says. "I've now become a with-it member of the computer generation."

"Just in case you don't know, it's the second generation already," Bubba Copeland shouts from the back of the room. "This is like saying you're with it because you have a telephone instead of a tin can and a string. Are you gonna wow us with the fact you're doing email now?"

"That and more," she says, ignoring the sarcasm. "My darling Hal gave me an iMac for my birthday. As you all must know, the new Macintosh is not a computer, it's a work of art. It's so stylish I'm displaying it on my coffee table in the living room. In its own way, it's as slim as I am."

"You're using it on the table, or just looking at it?" I ask.

"I sit on the sofa and lean forward, Ruby."

I can picture her aiming long fingernails at the stylish keys.

"We Mac owners are a special breed — surely in your business, you've noticed that."

"A breed apart, I hope," Bubba says.

"Enough, Bubba. I've decided we should have a website promoting our latkes. We can send orders all over the country."

"Let me get this straight," I say. "Are we selling advance orders for next Chanukah, or leftover orders from this one?"

"The latke, being a pancake, is as timeless as the potato," she says.

"And as boring. When do we get to vote on this loser?" Bubba says.

"There's always a market for Jewish culture, Bubba, and if you were more sophisticated you'd see that. We have to think big here. I can certainly tell you're not an Apple computer user."

"I get my electronics from Radio Shack, with the rest of the peons," he says. "And we don't eat latkes in January, either."

I guess Essie Sue gets the hint from the cheers Bubba receives. She switches gears fast, using her executive prerogative.

"I'm putting my cousin Zelda in charge of

a committee to explore the website idea," she says. "I don't need a vote for that. Zelda's a computer person. She works at Circuit City."

"She works the switchboard," Kevin says in my ear.

I hate getting publicly involved in Essie Sue's messes, but there's a point that needs making fast.

"Look," I say, "this fund-raising project was supposed to help pay for the choir trip this spring. If it's not going to work, I think we should drop it and think of some other ways to finance the conference expenses."

"You're a spoilsport, Ruby," she says. "I will not have you coming in here after this stunning slide presentation and demoralizing the congregation."

She glares at Bitsy, who seizes the moment and goes into meditation mode in the wink of a false eyelash.

"Let's all close our baby blues," she says. "Picture a white beach with lapping waves washing over you. I want you to think of that diastolic blood pressure number going down, down, down as you take yourself from this place and transport your psyche to Bermuda."

"What's wrong with the Dead Sea?" Bubba Copeland says. "You can float there, too. Israel needs the tourism."

"Okay, imagine whatever you like." Bitsy's no fool. "This is what I tell my grief-counseling clients, and it'll work for our dear distressed Ruby Rothman, too. Ruby, pretend you're melting into the pool of life, and that you've lost all boundaries between yourself and the universe. You can get this effect quicker with Prozac, but this is an emergency."

Essie Sue seconds that. "A definite emergency," she says. "You're a genius, Bitsy — worth every penny of what we're paying you. Get us back on track for the latke sales."

"How do you feel now, Ruby?" Bitsy asks, stretching a hand toward me.

"Like calling for a vote," I say. "Who'll second trashing the latke sales?"

"You mean all this counseling has been for nothing?" Essie Sue says. "You're hopelessly confused, Ruby. The meeting's adjourned. We'll discuss the sale another time."

Forget the Robert's Rules — Essie Sue knows what to do when she's outnumbered. I can't say the same for Bitsy — she gives a helpless glance at Essie Sue to make sure she's not being blamed for my failure to melt into the universe. The jury's out on that one, though — Essie Sue's headed out the door, leaving no clue as to what she's thinking about the results of the evening's boundary therapy.

Now that Essie Sue's out of here, the peace and love have departed from Bitsy's eyes, leaving cold appraisal in their wake as she glares at me.

"I guarantee you Prozac would do it," she says.

11

I've invited Rose to meet me at The Hot Bagel for lunch today — I have to be here anyway this afternoon to do the books. Since the business end of the bakery is my territory, with Milt handling the day-to-day operations, I'm able to set my own schedule most of the time. This has been an easy month so far, leaving me whole days free for my computer consulting.

"You don't look so hassled today, Ruby," Rose says as we sip some hot Lapsang Souchong tea. Neither of us is very hungry, and we're skipping bagel sandwiches to share a whitefish salad Milt's made for us.

I'm glad I appear calmer than usual, but I'm not about to tell Rose she's taken on all my agitation and more. She's drumming two broken nails on the table in a *pitty-pat* that's driving me crazy, and when she's not eating, she's twisting a strand of hair with her other hand. She's also doing that humming thing under her breath that she does unconsciously when she's stressed. I try to approach the situation in a more round-about way — which is not my style, and I'm never successful at it.

"And you?" I say.

"And me *what?*"

"Are you hassled?"

Well, there goes that subtlety.

"I guess my nervousness shows, huh?" she says.

"Oh, I don't know. I just sense you're on edge."

"Well, I am."

She dives into her salad so hard that the tines of her fork scrape through the lettuce to the bottom of her plate, screeching like a blackboard eraser.

"Okay, stop," I say. "Why don't you put down your fork and just tell me what's going on?"

"I've been thinking about Serena a lot since last week."

"After that weird memorial service, I'm not surprised. We never did get a good chance to talk about it."

"It left me feeling that I didn't know Serena as well as I thought I did. To tell you the truth, I always enjoyed making private fun of the other three quartet members when I was with Serena. Bart was a special case, since they were in the throes of a divorce — not much fun to be made there, I admit. But André and Irene were so full of themselves and so humorless about life in general that they were just asking to be taken down. I always thought Serena shared my view that they were both so serious they were comical, you know?"

"And she didn't share that?"

"I'm not certain now. They both sounded a lot closer to her than I thought they were."

"You can't be sure of that — they were probably trying to appear important at the memorial service. And since the dead can't respond, they felt safe in hinting at secrets with Serena that weren't there."

"Do you think?"

"I do. I wouldn't put any stock into what was said at that service."

"Okay, forget my doubts about them, Ruby. Aside from that, I don't understand about the heart thing, or problem, or whatever it was supposed to be. Serena had absolutely no history of heart disease, and her age and general state of health made it unlikely she'd drop dead like that. That happens more with middle-aged men, doesn't it? And she wasn't a smoker, and wasn't in the midst of violent exercise when she died."

"She was performing, Rose. That's a stressor of sorts."

"Before that crowd? They can't tell an alto from an Altoid. It's not as though her singing was being critiqued."

"Cardiac arrest does happen, Rose. And we checked with her internist — remember? He confirmed the diagnosis."

"Right. But you did want to know what was going on, and I took that to mean you were asking why I was on edge. That's why."

I don't think this lunch is helping her state of mind.

"What do you think could make you feel better about this, hon? It's over, and I hate to see you stuck in this emotional state. Mourning the loss of her friendship is one thing, but honestly, what else can you do?"

"It's too quick, Ruby. It's just too soon."

"Have you spoken with Serena's sister, Joellyn?"

"Several times. I finally got myself together enough to call her and offer my condolences last week. She was as shocked as I was. I called her again after the services here, just to tell her the nice things people said. She was very appreciative, and invited me to visit if I was ever in the area. She's called me twice since."

"That's unusual, isn't it? You've never met her?"

"No, but they didn't have much family, and she knows Serena was my friend. I think she just wants to talk with someone who knew Serena in her current life, if you know what I mean. She keeps asking me to visit. She can't bring herself to go through the belongings that were shipped to her."

"I know this seems off the wall, but have you considered going for a day or so? You could visit the cemetery together — maybe you'd feel some closure."

"It's expensive."

"Not if you get a weekend special off the Internet. I've seen fares as low as a hundred fifty round-trip, but you have to decide on the spot. And you wouldn't have expenses once you got there — she'll put you up, right?"

"Oh, yeah, no problem about that. She said she has a guest room and everything, and would pick me up at the airport."

"So she's really pushing for it, right?"

"Apparently."

"Want me to do the Net shopping for you? I'm on the email list for bargains from Austin to wherever."

"Let me call Joellyn and see how receptive she'd be to a spur-of-the-moment visitor, and then we'll see. Ray and Jackie could do without me for two days."

I have no idea if this is a good plan or not, but I do know that Rose's fingers aren't drumming the table anymore.

12

"We're like those couples with a double sink," I say. Paul and I are standing in front of my gas stove, each cooking on a different burner.

"Only this is sexier than brushing our teeth together," he says.

"I didn't know you thought of cooking as sexy," I say.

"With you it is." By way of illustration, he plucks a fat mushroom from his sauté pan, cools it in the air so it won't burn me, and plops it into my mouth.

"Umm . . . I can taste the garlic and ginger . . . that's positively orgasmic, now that I think of it."

I'm poaching the salmon in my pan, and he's sautéing the most luscious vegetables in his.

"Soon they'll be nestling together over here," he says, bending toward me to try the salmon I'm offering. I kiss him before letting him taste if the fish is done.

"So which is better," I say, "me or the salmon?"

"Right now? You," he says, "but remember, we haven't put it in my delicious sauce yet. Ask me later."

I only have the Key West souvenir pot holder to throw at him at the moment. It displays the recipe for the Key Lime pie I've made for our dessert.

"Keep that up and there'll be no later," I say.

I forget that Oy Vey's waiting by the stove for any goodies that might drop from our cooking pots. The poor thing makes a lunge for the pot holder because it's carrying such delicious odors, and gets nothing but a mouthful of cloth. Which she promptly shares with Chutzpah, and they go off into the living room to make a game of it.

"They've eaten the pie on the pot holder," Paul says, "so you'll have to give me the real thing."

He's wearing a new gray sweatshirt with old gray sweatpants that would match if they weren't so faded, his beard is a day old, and he's without a doubt the sexiest man I've seen in this town. Between the workouts he does to keep in shape as a cop, and the fact that he's naturally lean and lithe, Paul's a hottie. I can hardly keep my hands off him, but they're occupied culinarily at the moment, which I'm telling myself is a good thing. We're still taking things easy.

"Are we going to set the table with the watermelon place mats I brought you?" he says.

We have a *tacky* thing going — whenever either of us sees something especially outrageous, we buy it as a gift for the other. Until tonight, he hadn't been able to top the Elvis-Pelvis salt-and-pepper shakers I gave him. But his plastic place mats cut in the shape of watermelons — a tribute to my house on Watermelon Lane — may have tipped the balance.

"I was thinking of candlelight and white linen," I say, "but since I don't want to hurt your feelings, I'll forgo the romance and use the plastic."

"No, maybe we should save the watermelon mats for breakfast and go for your choice — especially with this great dinner."

"How do you know you'll be here for breakfast?" I can't resist saying.

"I don't know, maybe it's in the stars. The receptionist at the station house told us the planets were aligned in love mode this month. I wanted to be sure and remember to tell you that."

"Because you're so into that, right? Admit it, the only signs you care about are the thirty-five-mile-per-hour speed trap signs all over Eternal."

"Rats. I told her the horoscope shit wouldn't work with you."

"Wrong. It's all working, sweetie, can't you tell that? I think you're adorable to-night."

"Only tonight? Not all the time?"

Just as I'm thinking we should get the salad out of the refrigerator, the phone rings. I look quickly at the caller ID and see that it's a call from Ohio.

"Should I answer it?" I say, after telling Paul it must be Rose phoning from Joellyn's house.

"Wonder what she wants?" he says.

"Your call," I say. "What should I do?"

"Answer it and I'll put the fish in the sauce for a few minutes."

"Okay, but remember that salmon can overcook fast."

I pick up the phone on the last ring before the machine answers.

"Hi, Rose," I say.

"Oh, you know it's me already."

"Miracles of modern electronics. How's it going there? Is Joellyn with you?"

I'm thinking we might have a more frank conversation if she's by herself. Not that it makes much difference.

"She's right here, and she says hi."

"Are you two having a good visit?"

I'm really torn — this is the worst possible time for a call, and if it were anyone but Rose on the other end, I'd phone back later. But I'm sure she's not calling just for a chat. We're close, but not enough for her to call from Ohio just to say hello.

"What's up?" I say, then instantly regret sounding so businesslike — I don't want to hurry her. I'm just finding myself distracted by the muscles in Paul's back. And he's moving around my kitchen as if he owns it.

In spite of myself, I put my hand over the mouthpiece and ask him if I should tell her I'll call back.

"Better see what she wants," he says.

As if to contradict any sense of urgency, Rose gives me an accounting of the two days she and Joellyn have spent together.

"It's been good for both of us," she says. "Neither of us felt any closure after Serena's death, and we're enjoying remembering her together. Me, especially — I didn't know much about their childhood. And we're looking at old photos, too."

I can see our romantic dinner slipping

away as we speak, even though Paul's making good use of the time by setting the table.

"I'm really glad you're enjoying one another," I say. "Paul's here, too — I'll tell him." Maybe that'll get her to the point.

"Uh-oh. Is it dinnertime there? I should have waited an hour."

She should have waited until tomorrow, but that's just me being selfish.

"Lieutenant Lundy's there," I hear Rose tell Joellyn.

There's more murmuring on their end, and then another voice on the phone.

"Ruby, this is Joellyn. I'm wondering if you'd mind if I speak to Paul for a minute?"

"Sure," I say. She doesn't sound in the mood for small talk, so I don't make any. Although I have to admit I'm a bit surprised at how abrupt she is, considering all the futzing around Rose has been doing.

"She wants you," I say, waving the phone in his direction. "It's Joellyn — the sister."

Paul gets on the phone, and I see what I can do to salvage dinner, which has been simmering. I turn off the gas burner, assuming the damage has already been done, and take out a bottle of Pinot Grigio I've been chilling. Then, before I put it on the table, I decide to return it to the refrigerator again. Who knows how long he'll be?

It's a good thing, because he spends the next few minutes in total silence while Joellyn is apparently filling him in on whatever they called about. This is, of course, my tiny version of hell, since not only am I not sharing this candlelight dinner with Paul, but I'm missing out on whatever's going on. And if I hadn't mentioned that Paul was here, they'd have been telling all this to me, not him.

"When is Rose planning on coming home?" I hear him finally say. "Then why don't you have her bring it on the plane with her. And just for safekeeping, can you put the files on a CD and send it to me by FedEx? Do you know how to burn one? If not, I don't want you to risk losing them altogether."

The answer he gets apparently satisfies him, because he relaxes enough to sit down on one of the kitchen chairs while he talks. Then he stands up again.

"Look, since you're computer savvy, why not do a third thing? Send me the files as an attachment, too. After you burn the CD. Send it tonight to my email address at police headquarters."

As he gives her the particulars, I'm seeing the romance go out the window. Maybe I'm just catastrophizing, but Paul has that all-business look he gets when new information comes in. And then there was that reference to the email tonight.

I'm as nuts as Paul is — now that he's hanging up, I'm as interested in what's going on in Ohio as I am in dinner.

"Let's eat," he says. "I know this came at the wrong time." He brushes my cheek with his lips as he heads for the stove. "Do you think the salmon's still edible?"

I squash my curiosity until we light the candles, pour the wine, sit down, and try the food — which isn't bad, but not what we'd hoped for. Just as I'm about to ask something, he beats me to it.

"Joellyn received Serena's personal effects," he says, "including her laptop. She decided to go through the contents of it with Rose, who's a lot more familiar with Serena's life here in Eternal than Joellyn is. They ran into some disturbing material in several Notes files Serena kept, and they think I should see them."

"Look, hon," I say. "I know this is going to be on your mind tonight. Why don't we finish dinner and then use my computer to access your email from here? It might not be what we'd planned, but we can at least take a look at the stuff, and maybe afterwards, you can still stay over."

"Thanks for understanding," he says. "Joellyn asked me to keep it to myself for now. I need to look at the material down at headquarters in case I have to access any databases."

"By yourself?"

"Uh-huh."

"No way. Rose called my house, interrupted my dinner date — well, *our* dinner date — and had no idea you'd be here. She would have obviously told me the whole thing."

"Maybe so, but the deceased's blood relation, her own sister, told me unequivocally to keep this confidential until she and I can discuss it. When she found me, she obviously changed her mind about telling you."

I get it, but I don't have to like it.

"That's not fair. You and I talk about things like this all the time — you understand I'm reliable."

"Which is beside the point, and you know it. You're just disappointed, and I don't blame you. I am, too. But what do you expect me to do — betray the woman's confidence?"

I finish my glass of wine. Then Paul does something I *really* hate him for.

"Look," he says. "Why don't I pick up the email tomorrow? We'll have our evening tonight. It won't kill me to wait."

I sit there, twirling the salad greens with my fork, and then I have to crack a smile in spite of myself.

"Yeah, but it'll kill me, and you damn well know it. The sooner you find out what's in that laptop, the sooner I can learn about it. Somehow."

He takes my hands across the table and kisses the inside of each.

"Tell me," I say. "You knew what my reaction would be when you made the offer to wait, didn't you?"

"Let's just say I know who I'm dealing with," he says. "That's why I'm good at what I do."

"Oh, you're good at what you do, all right — you just don't do it with me."

He stands me up and pulls me to him.

"Look at me," he says. "Do you have any doubt whatsoever about how I feel about you? And don't you dare lie for effect."

After he leaves, when I'm eating the cold salmon and finishing the wine, I think to myself that Ed couldn't have pulled this off in a thousand years.

13

"We aren't getting the advance latke orders we need to finance the trip, Ruby — not even with the website."

Essie Sue's waiting for me on my front porch as I drive in from my early morning aerobics class.

"I'm sorry about that, Essie Sue, but why did you hit *me* up at this ungodly hour?"

She's wearing her immaculate winter white pantsuit, and staring at my leotard and the sneakers I untied in the car to give my feet some breathing room.

"Honestly, Ruby, your grooming leaves something to be desired."

Apparently, my appearance is taking precedence over whatever it was she came over here to harass me about.

"If you don't like my grooming, Essie Sue, then why don't you give me time to groom? I just left the gym to come home and take a shower. And why do I need to give you an explanation anyhow? You're the one barging into my morning, not the other way around."

She follows me into the house, taking great pains to avoid Oy Vey and Chutzpah, who aren't getting near her, anyway. They have long memories.

I lead her onto the deck in back, where she stands up until I find her a towel to put down on the chaise.

"It's cold out here. Why do you use your deck in the winter, anyway?"

"Because we live in the Sunbelt?"

"Don't be cute, Ruby. I wouldn't be over here if I weren't desperate. You're a computer expert, so tell me why our temple website isn't producing a bigger yield?"

"How many orders have come in?"

"Two. And that's worldwide. I want you to fix it."

"I hate to break it to you, but this isn't a computer problem, Essie Sue."

"So *what's wrong?*"

"Like maybe the rest of the world isn't grabbed by the idea of ordering latkes two months after Chanukah? I told you this wouldn't work. You got great response from the congregation, so take it and run."

"I would, but that money's already been spent paying for Bitsy. I had much bigger plans than the local scene."

"You had no plans other than putting this on the website. You could never have filled the orders, even if they had come in — that takes cooking, freezing, mailing — none of which you were prepared for."

"You sound just like the man at the health department — he said he was going to be watching me like a hawk to make sure we were sanitary. Just because we had a few problems with those matzo ball sales a few years ago."

Now I remember why this whole idea had me shuddering — the matzo ball fiasco. I bring us mugs of hot coffee from the kitchen.

"So the health department was on your back, too? You never told me that."

"Forget it, Ruby. Let's have a rummage sale. Otherwise, you people will never have enough to get to Canada."

"The choir has already knocked itself out on this project. Why not use some of that money you've got socked away in that rainy day account? It's earning about one percent interest."

Essie Sue has a habit of squirreling away the proceeds of her fund-raising projects instead of using them for their intended purposes. I have no idea how much she has, but I'm acting on my hunch that there's plenty there.

"You mean my emergency funds?"

"I mean the temple's funds — there's a difference. You can always replenish them later."

"I'll think about it. But only if the participants increase the portion they pay out of pocket for the trip."

I *am* starting to get cold out here.

"I don't mean to be inhospitable, but since you invited yourself over here, are we finished now? I have to get to work soon."

"Just one more thing. The rabbi told me you were still seeing that policeman. I have an idea to get you out of this."

"I don't remember telling anyone I wanted out of it — whatever the meaning of *it* is."

"Don't go Clintonian on me, Ruby. As someone close to you, I have an interest in your welfare. My cousin Claire in California told me about a fabulous love-connection website full of nice Jewish men. It's called Nu — a Jew for You. Since you're on the computer all the time, I thought of you right away. I got you a guest membership, which allows you to browse the selection of men without giving your real name. They call it *lurking.*"

They call it *losers.* Oy.

"No thanks, Essie Sue. I like to look my poison right in the eye from the beginning."

"Oh, they have photos included. You can see the potential partners."

"Don't you remember those stories of the men who sent their mail-order brides pictures of movie stars instead of themselves? This stuff's been going on forever."

"Ruby, you're so naive. It's totally kosher certified. By online rabbis, I think."

"I think not. But, gee, thanks anyway. Let me walk you through the yard to your car."

I usher Essie Sue into her driver's seat, relieved that she at least agreed to leave when I asked her to.

"You'll be getting your first email from these people tomorrow," she yells as she drives off. "Start composing your bio."

14

Email to: Nan
From: Ruby
Subject: Catch-up

I can't remember what I told you on the phone and what I wrote in email, but here goes. I don't believe I'm admitting this, but we only have a few weeks before leaving for Canada, and I still haven't been able to wrangle any information from Paul or Rose concerning what was on Serena's laptop. I do understand that Paul gave his word, but I don't see why Rose hasn't told me herself. Paul doesn't want to get in the middle here, but he thinks Serena's sister Joellyn wants to keep it quiet, and must have made Rose promise. At any rate, it's frustrating, and Rose seems to be avoiding me.

On the phone you said there might be nothing much to tell, but I know from something I overheard this week that Paul's giving Joellyn advice on how to get the body exhumed. As you know professionally, permission for exhumation isn't an easy process, and it certainly isn't a speedy one. But Joellyn's also a paralegal, so she knows her way through the legal forms involved.

Paul's also asked me not to go on the Lake Louise trip, which of course makes me think people from the choir are involved in all this — not that I have any idea how. He probably thinks I'll ask a zillion questions of them once we get out of town. Which I won't, of course, if he'll just *tell* me something.

Email to: Ruby
From: Nan
Subject: Cat and mouse?

So let me see if I've got this straight. You're trying to use the trip as leverage to get more information out of Paul, right? You're figuring that if he doesn't want you to go but refuses to say why, then you *will* go. And if he's worried enough, he'll tell you what's going on in order to keep you home and safe.

You do realize that you could both be losers here. He's pursuing the one path which will ensure that you go, because you're like a two-year-old when someone says no to you, and you're embarking on a dangerous journey if you travel with these people not knowing what you're doing. In other words, the usual. And now you've got me worried, too. Maybe I should call Paul myself and explain the more unattractive aspects of your character.

Email to: Nan
From: Ruby
Subject: Threats can backfire

Ha . . . if you call Paul, you'll leave yourself open to charges that you're interested in him yourself. I distinctly remember giving you a chance if you wanted it. Now, of course, I'm so into him that I couldn't possibly make that offer, but that won't stop me from using it against you.

Email to: Ruby
From: Nan
Subject: Not buying it

Good try, but I'm still worried about you. Keep your man, jealous as I am, and I'll struggle along in my single state.

Email to: Nan
From: Ruby
Subject: I've got just the thing for you

Essie Sue signed me up with a pseudonym on some dating website called Nu — a Jew for You. She doesn't think Paul's a suitable match. I refused to go on there so she's picking up the responses herself, which she can do since she's the paying customer there, not me. I do know that it's trendy to explore online dating these days and that they're not all losers, but I'm not giving her any encouragement. It's still smoke and mirrors to me.

15

Tonight Kevin's asked me over to his apartment, AKA Gym Central, since the so-called furnishings are leftovers Essie Sue gave him from the health spa she used to own. He never asks me to his place unless he's in trouble, so I'm wary. Just so it won't be a total loss, I figure I can work out on his treadmill while he's filling me in.

"Why are you wearing those spandex bicycle pants?" he asks me as he opens the door.

"Hello to you, too," I say, bumping into the ab machine he uses as a coffee table. "You don't like my exercise outfit?"

"Is that what it is?"

"I thought it would match your equipment," I say.

"Oh, that. I don't even notice it anymore. I just use it to put things on. And the reclining bike seat is pretty comfortable next to my reading lamp."

"You realize you could sell this stuff and furnish your whole apartment," I say.

"No, I couldn't. Essie Sue gave it to me, and she thinks I use it. She's the reason I asked you over, Ruby."

I slump down on the bench-press seat and put my feet up on the elliptical trainer. It's not comfortable, but I've plunked myself down in worse places. When Essie Sue's involved, things get complicated fast, so I'm dreading the rest of this.

"Want an energy bar?"

"No, thanks." Kevin's skills as a host are exceeded only by his constant attempts to get rid of the stale supplies Essie Sue unloaded on him from the health spa. These bars have to be years old by now, and I've learned the hard way to avoid them.

"Don't get comfortable," he says. "I want you to come into the bedroom so I can show you something."

Despite the fact that Kevin's had crushes on me in the past, invitations to his bedroom don't faze me. In fact, I welcome the chance to lie on his bed — the only real piece of furniture he owns.

"My computer's in here," he says, "but I guess you remember that."

And so it is, securely resting on the seat of a biceps builder.

"I can see it here from the bed," I say, deciding that if I'm not going to get a workout, I might as well relax in indolence. "It's not broken, is it?"

"No, I didn't ask you over to fix anything."

That's a relief. As a computer consultant, I've had friendships ruined by social invitations masking desperation calls for free advice. I don't mind helping friends in the least — it's their not being honest that bothers me. I hate those "Oh, by the way, can you look at this software?" comments I get as soon as I walk in the door.

"So what's the problem?" I ask Kevin.

"I want you to please go online with me and help me deal with these women who're responding to my ad. I don't know any of them, and already some of them are trying to date me. Or worse."

"You wrote an ad? This is a side of you I don't know, guy."

"That's a side of me I don't know either. Essie Sue did it. And now I have to deal with it."

"Oy. She signed you up on the Nu — a Jew for You site? Just ignore it. She threatened to do it for me, too, but I'm pretending this never happened. Since my name isn't on the bio, I decided to let her handle things. If I don't go on there, it'll all go away sooner or later, and she'll get tired of paying the fees."

"But that's just it — she told me she'd paid a lot to sign me up. She's not your boss, Ruby — I can't ignore her the way you do. Since she has my password, she's seen all the interest in me online, and she wants me to explore some of these contacts."

"She's not entitled to control your personal life, Kevin."

"Yeah, right. She talked me up to Bitsy and now I can't get rid of her. I told Essie Sue I wasn't interested in Bitsy, so she says she's making up for it by fixing me up online."

"Whoa, come sit on the bed, Kevin, where I can see more than your back. I had no idea you had all these relationship problems."

"Yeah, with no relationships. Just tsuris. Trouble plus."

"Okay, first things first. I thought you kind of liked Bitsy. Last I heard, she'd asked you for a date."

"She's too pushy, and she scares me a little. I told her to find somebody else — that I wasn't sure about us."

"So how did that go over?"

"Badly. Now she ignores me."

"Well, what do you expect her to do? You need to fish or cut bait."

"I'm not fishing."

"Okay, so be glad she's ignoring you. Although I'll bet she's just regrouping. But what's the deal with these virtual romances? Are you really just doing what Essie Sue wants, or are you interested?"

"I'm kind of fascinated in one way. And in another, I don't like those women jumping to conclusions about me. Look at my bio and tell me what you think."

"She did the bio, not you?"

"Uh-huh." Kevin's now curled up on the bed in a fetal position. I know from past experience this means he wants me to take over big-time.

He's already logged on, so I go over to the biceps-building machine and take a look.

I skip over the curriculum vitae, which she's apparently taken directly from the form Kevin submitted to the temple. If this doesn't turn anyone off, nothing will. But I'm still curious as to why he's attracted so many women, so I continue with the introductory questions she's answered for him.

Describe Yourself
ANSWER: Somewhere between Brad Pitt and Robert Redford before he got old.

Yep, vintage Essie Sue.

Why You Should Want to Go Out with Me
ANSWER: My exciting sexual nature, my muscular body, my large brain, and my clever repartee.

Where I'd Rather Be Right Now
ANSWER: On a romantic beach with you or in shul.

Last Two Books I've Read
ANSWER: *Life of Maimonides* and *Sex and the Single Man.*

Favorite Songs
ANSWER: "Love Me Tender" and "Hatikvah."

Worldly Goods
ANSWER: Extremely comfortable and willing to share.

Ten Things I Can't Live Without
ANSWER: The Commandments.

Okay, I have to come up for air. I don't know quite what to say as I turn to Kevin on the bed.

"So what do you think, Ruby?" He's

uncoiled himself and is now stretched out and leaning on one elbow.

"Let's say it's a perfect illustration of all the things I've ever envisioned about online romance, Kevin."

"Wait until you read the responses," he says. "These women are voracious."

"I must truly say that I cannot begin to imagine what kind of person would be attracted to Essie Sue's creation here."

"Some of them say they're beautiful and wealthy, Ruby. And sexy. And want me."

"If you're thinking of getting involved, why don't you just go on there with your own description of yourself?"

"I thought of that, but it would be a lot more boring than hers."

Hmm. I can't say I disagree with him.

"Why don't I show you a couple of the really good responses," he says.

"Be my guest," I say as I change places with him. "Just read them to me."

"Okay, here's one woman who looks promising. Certainly better than Bitsy. She's more my type — not so *cutesy.*"

Describe Yourself
ANSWER: Iím sultry, sensual, and ready to introduce you to my special brand of love. Iíve been extremely lucky so far in my

choice of men — the Greek god type has always been attracted to me, and I'm sure you will be no exception. I will know your every need.

"See, Ruby, this woman is a fantasy of mine — someone who'd be all over me and I wouldn't have to do much."

I'm not sure I want to be this close to Kevin's fantasy life, but what the hell. I can't leave him in this wonder world without some healthy hints — kind of like an Héloïse of broadband.

"Uh, Kevin, you should know right off that if all these gods are surrounding this woman, how does she have the time to seduce you?"

"Well, she is a little overt. I don't like women who come on too strong. This is why it's scary. But she's not all about sex — she's very smart. Listen to this:

What More You Should Know About Me
ANSWER: Warning — don't respond to this ad if you're not willing to ferret out all my brainteasers — this will indicate whether your level of intelligence matches mine. Prepare to be bombarded by questions as to your hopefully esoteric tastes in literature, film, music, drama, and TV. Can you

keep up with me on the cleverness level?

"See, Ruby? She must have quite an intelligence quotient."

"I'd say she rates pretty high on the dominatrix scale, too. Do you really want an Essie Sue on hormones?"

"She can't hurt me online. Help me write something back to her. Who knows — I might be one of those Greek gods she's talking about."

It's time for me to crawl off Fantasy Island here on Kevin's mattress and go home to Oy Vey and Chutzpah, who are suddenly looking healthy, sane, and stable.

"I'm sure you'll come up with something clever, Kevin," I say as I avoid the stationary bicycle by the bedroom door and head back to Watermelon Lane. I think I'll watch a sitcom Kevin isn't starring in.

16

Carl Harn, my neighbor three doors down, is retrieving his wet morning paper from the grass as Oy Vey and I jog by.

"They didn't double-bag it again, Ruby." He holds up a soggy clump of newsprint, and I try to convey sympathy without having to break my stride. He's used to my multitasking, and we both wave as I pass.

"Call Toby," I yell back at him, but I know he won't, which is why our latest news carrier gets away with murder — no one takes the time to complain. I continue my conversation with Oy Vey as we run — since I'm no sprinter, she has no trouble keeping up with me on her three legs.

"This is the day," I tell her. "If Paul won't talk to me about Rose's visit to Ohio, I'm going straight to the source."

Since the look she throws me signals agreement, I speed-dial Rose on my cell phone before I lose my nerve. I'll have a better chance of getting her at the start of the day before we both get busy.

"Hi," I say when she answers, "I hope this isn't too early, but I know it's useless to get you on the phone at night."

"Yeah," she says, "Jackie pretty much takes over with her school friends from the afternoon on. We've thought of getting her an extra line, but it seems indulgent."

"Good luck on holding out," I say, knowing her daughter's powers of persuasion. "I'm calling —"

"I know why, Ruby, and before you start I want to apologize. We were supposed to get together when I came back from visiting Joellyn in Ohio, but I've been so backed up that I knew I couldn't make a definite date with you, and I guess that kept me from calling. Not a pretty picture."

"Look, I don't mind, Rose. I realize what the last few months have been like for you. But how about now? Have you caught up a bit? There are things I need to talk to you about before I leave for Canada."

"Canada? Is the conference coming up already? I can't believe the time's gone by so quickly — thank goodness I backed out early. Another trip is all I need right now. By the way, what's that hissing noise I hear on your end?"

"That's not hissing, it's me panting. I'm trying to talk to you and jog at the same time."

"Do you want to call back?"

Oh, no, you don't. I'm not taking the chance of getting your answering machine one more time.

"No, let's make a date now. Can I come over for a quick cup of coffee later this morning?"

"Everything's a mess here, Ruby. Meet me at Bowery Road Grill."

"What time?"

"Let's make it just before noon — maybe we can get a table then."

"Okay, see you there, Rose. Bye."

Jackpot. I think I caught her by surprise, before she had a chance to make excuses she's not a morning person, either. And I'll be sure not to answer if she tries to call and cancel. She won't have the nerve to phone the restaurant once I'm there to say she's not coming.

"We did it, Oy Vey," I say as we make it to our front door. "This'll take the pressure off Paul, too."

I'd like to grab another cup of coffee, but I decide to jump in the shower first. I hear the phone ring while I'm still washing my hair, so of course I don't answer it. But then the caller starts the whole ringing cycle again. No one does this but Kevin.

Sure enough, when I check the caller ID later, it displays the Temple Rita number. He can wait until I get my coffee. Kevin's vision of my home life is that I'm never out — that I sit by the phone screening calls, especially his. His response is never to leave a message, but to hang up and dial me again. And again. I guess his theory is that I'll think the call is so urgent I'll pick up.

I settle down in the living room with the morning paper and a mug of Kenya, black. I don't have that much time before meeting Rose for an early lunch, so coffee's all I'm allowing myself. Kevin's at it again, though, and I might as well get this over with.

"Ruby, it's me."

"Yeah, I gathered that. I feel as if we're still having our conversation from last night, Kevin, and that I never went home."

"Well, you could have stayed if you'd wanted."

I'm not about to make the subtle *unsubtle,* so I don't pursue this.

"And this call is about — ?"

"There's a complication with my social life, Ruby."

"What's the matter? Is one of your online lovers hopping on a plane for Eternal?

Maybe Essie Sue shouldn't make you sound so irresistible, Kevin."

"No, this involves something right here. Remember I told you Bitsy the party planner was ignoring me? Now I find out she still wants to date me."

"Yes, you said you were ambivalent about it, and I was encouraging you. Now that these online women are coming for you out of the ether, I think it's even more important that you do some romancing in real time. Call her for a date."

"That won't be necessary. Adrian, the new temple secretary, tells me Bitsy signed up to be my roommate on the trip to Canada. We're all supposed to double up to save money, and I assumed I'd be rooming with a man."

"I didn't know that — no one's called me about doubling up. But as for Bitsy rooming with you, that's ridiculous. Just call and tell her no. Unless you want to."

"I haven't even gone out with her, Ruby. This is moving too fast."

"Then tell Adrian to take your name off the list as her roommate, and then to call Bitsy and tell her to make other arrangements. Since Bitsy didn't even ask you, you don't owe her a personal call, either. But be sure Adrian lets her know you're not available."

"I knew you'd figure something out, Ruby. Thanks."

"Don't mention it. If that's all you wanted, I have to get off the phone now."

"Uh, Ruby — one more thing you don't seem to know about. I'm not sure how to put this to you."

"Put what?"

"Well, Adrian also said Hal wasn't going along on the Canada trip, and that Essie Sue signed herself up as your roommate."

17

No way am I sleeping in the same room with Essie Sue Margolis. First, I'm shocked that she'd even consider not having a private suite, much less want to room with *moi*. Not that I have much time to obsess about Kevin's call this morning — I'll save that for tonight. At the moment it's all I can do to keep the speedometer down as I try to make it on time to Bowery Road Grill, a favorite of Rose's. The restaurant's located in a small renovated home, and I have to admit it makes up in charm for what it lacks in variety. Of course, I should talk — The Hot Bagel's menu is even more limited, but then, it's a bagelry.

"Ruby, you're the only person who could entice me to lunch in the middle of a week like this," she says as we're led to a table by the window.

"I'm glad I snared you at all," I say. "I thought you'd gone underground."

I'm still somewhat miffed that Rose has ignored me since coming home, busy schedule or not. She was over at my house almost daily after Serena died, and I was glad I could help comfort her. I was the one who gave her the push to visit Serena's sister. Then, after the trip, *nada*. Still, I shouldn't lose patience just yet. She's had a difficult time.

After we order the chef salads they've specialized in since the fifties, I imagine that I'm lighting up a cigarette, and wait for her to say something. It's a trick I learned in my twenties, and it seems to be the precise amount of time needed to give the other person a chance to speak without pressure.

Only she doesn't, and I feel I have to charge in to the rescue.

"So have you felt better or worse since seeing Joellyn?" I say. "I can imagine either."

"I felt better learning more about Serena's life while I was there, but the uncertainty has me on edge now."

"In what way?"

"Well, I guess Paul's told you that the family's having the body exhumed, or trying to."

"I did hear that, but not from Paul, actually."

"I did ask him to keep this quiet, but I

suspected he might tell you."

"No, Rose, honey. Anything you decide to share will have to come from you, not Paul — that's just who he is. I was hoping, though, that you *would* want to take me into your confidence. There's no question that the information would be safe with me — I think you know that. On the other hand, if you feel you can't, I'll understand that, too. What I really wanted was for you to tell me directly one way or the other."

"I should have touched base with you, especially after all the help you offered at a time when I needed it. And I do know I can trust you."

"As long as you're sure of that, I'm satisfied."

We eat silently for a minute or two, although I'm mainly just picking at my hard-boiled egg.

"It was just so weird, Ruby. Joellyn and I read Serena's laptop notes together, and it was as if I were eavesdropping on someone I didn't know. It's been embarrassing — I think that's why I found it hard to talk about. But here goes."

"Look, I'm feeling uncomfortable about this, too," I say. "I'm sure the details will all be made public sooner or later, and as long as I know I have your trust, I honestly don't mind not knowing. I feel better just having you explain this much."

"But I don't feel better. I'm feeling frustrated, and I'm beginning to think I really need to tell you everything. Paul suggested that I might want to get your advice because you have this bottom-line way of approaching things. He thought you'd make a good sounding board."

"Really? He didn't say anything to me." That's Paul, of course — he wouldn't. But it would be his way — not only to give Rose an outlet she needed, but to fill me in before the Canada trip.

"So what happened? Were there lots of notes? Emails?"

"You're bottom-lining already, Ruby." Rose is digging into her salad all of a sudden as if she's really enjoying it. Maybe she does need to unload.

"Notes," she says. "Mostly Serena had written notes to herself, like a journal, except that they were written more randomly. She kept them in a file called, of all things, 'Spiritual.' "

"Huh? That doesn't sound like Serena."

"That's what I'm trying to tell you. None of this is like Serena."

"Start from the beginning. These were chronological, I assume. Like a diary?"

"It wasn't a diary. But, yes, we did start reading the earliest notes first, trying to find some unifying factor."

"And did you? Were they especially *spiritual?*"

"They centered around a few subjects — one was a particular person, and the others were about a group and an idea."

"I have the feeling you're dancing around this, Rose. What's the deal?"

"I know I'm not doing a very good job of explaining this. Let me approach it from a different angle."

"That would help," I say. "But get it out."

"Let me put it this way — did you happen to know that Serena was having an affair with André Korman?"

I choke on the anchovies.

"Yeah, I know," Rose says, "it's something of a shock."

"Are you sure?" I say. "She didn't seem the type."

"What's the type when you think about it, Ruby? All kinds of people have affairs, and most of them are big secrets. These files chronicle their meetings, the times she saw him, wanted to see him, didn't see him, didn't want to see him — the whole megillah."

"Do you think Bart knew? Or that it had

something to do with their divorcing?"

"I doubt it. Don't forget that André was married at the time and still is — they'd have wanted things private."

"So what *was* the timing, Rose?"

"It didn't happen until after her divorce, although as you say, I guess we can't be absolutely sure that the attraction didn't start while she was still with Bart."

"Bart left Serena, not the other way around, right?"

"Yes, she seemed extremely upset at the time."

"Meaning that this could have been a fling in retaliation, after the fact. Maybe she just wanted Bart to know he didn't wring all the life out of her."

"The reasons don't really matter, though, do they? It happened."

We both take a breather from this shocker — I can hardly eat anything, but Rose is still hungry. Of course, she's used to this news by now and I'm not.

"Hey," I say, giving up on the salad, "tell me what's spiritual about this affair. You did say that's what she named the file, didn't you?"

"That's where it all gets weird. In one of the chapters or sections or whatever they were, Serena talks about the deeper regions of Jewish thought. From what her sister and I could gather, she and André and a couple of other people in the choir had formed a study group."

"You mean Madonna Kaballah or the real thing? Jewish mysticism's also a fad now. Surely it couldn't be the deeper stuff — that's not something to dabble in without direction."

"I have no idea what it was, but I do know André was the initiator and the group was small — all women, I think."

"That figures. Was he sleeping with all of them?"

"I don't get any indication of that. He and Serena were hiding the affair from the group, too, or at least they thought they were."

"I'll bet André would plotz if he knew Serena had written any of this down."

"Yes, his worst nightmare. His wife's inheritance supports their fairly lavish lifestyle, you know — he's certainly not getting rich from the health food store."

"Now I can see why Joellyn's optimistic about getting permission for the exhumation. Although nothing about this file adds up to more than slimy behavior, obviously."

"No, there was one other thing Joellyn and I read that I haven't told you about. It was the last entry Serena made."

We're paying the waiter by this time because I have work to do this afternoon, and Rose waits until he leaves before continuing. Mentally, I'm halfway out the door, so I'm taken totally by surprise.

"She says in this final section, 'They're frightening me.' "

"That's all?"

"Just those words. Maybe someone was threatening her."

"It could be the Kabbalah that was frightening to her, Rose. The mysticism the Kabbalists were exploring was known to be so complex that no one below middle age was allowed to study those subjects. And André isn't exactly a subtle guy. He was probably laying it on just to impress — the scarier the better."

"I hope you're right, Ruby. Because if it wasn't the Kabbalah, then Serena was afraid of something much more concrete."

18

This is my favorite way to talk to Paul when I'm not with him — surrounded by my warm down comforter and three pillows, Oy Vey and Chutzpah sleeping at the foot of the bed. A steaming mug of Constant Comment is on the side table ready for sipping when it cools, and the cordless phone is snuggled under my ear.

"You were a doll to encourage Rose to confide in me," I say.

"I thought it would help her as well as you," he says. "She seemed to be losing her grip for a while after she came back from Ohio. Since I knew it would take time for Joellyn to negotiate her way through the exhumation process, I wasn't sure Rose could hold out."

"I just like the way you do things, honey. You were patient with both of us and still managed to be professional. I wanted you to know it didn't escape me."

"Thanks. I also had a selfish purpose — now I can kick this back and forth with you. So what did you think?"

"Serena was afraid — there's no doubt about that. And I'm as surprised as Rose was about the affair. Since André's the last person I'd find attractive, I can't be objective about this, but I thought Serena had better taste. On the other hand, he seems pretty confident, so I suppose he must have had some measure of success with women. Do you think he could be that good in bed?"

"I really wouldn't know, honey — I'll leave that speculation to you. I can tell you, though, from years of police experience, that you can never second-guess another person's private obsessions. If Serena was hooked on him, it could have been for reasons only her shrink would understand. Luckily, all we have to do is accept it as fact."

"Well, she makes it perfectly clear, doesn't she? Unless you think there was coercion involved."

"Nope. It was mutual — the notes make that apparent."

"Paul, I have an idea. You probably won't like it."

I taste my tea, and the aroma's fabulous.

"Can you see why you drive me so crazy, Ruby?"

"No."

"It's that way you have of preparing me for something you've already decided to do. If you know I won't like whatever this is, then why not do me a favor and forget it?"

"You mean, not mention it? You said you like me to be up front with you."

"No, I mean forget it, not hide it — you know damn well that's what I meant. Just go my way for once."

"At least listen to my idea, okay? I'm thinking that the trip will be a great chance for me to get closer to this group. Serena indicated that choir members were involved. We're spending hours on the train trip through the Canadian Rockies, and you know how good I am at this. I promise I'll find out something."

"Yeah, I do know — too good for your *own* good, if past experience is any indicator. This is a closed environment, and it could be dangerous. Serena sensed it, and she was apparently in the in-group. So why would they ever trust you, of all people? You're not even friends with them."

"But I can be. And this isn't the only group on the train. Half the temple leadership is going along, plus others who're headed for the ChoirFest. Hey, did you hear that Essie Sue wants me to room with her? A joke, right?"

"Don't try to distract me. Although if you insist on attending when I'd rather have you stay home, I think it would be perfect to have someone like Essie Sue keeping an eye on you. At least I'd know you couldn't get too far out of her orbit — she wouldn't stand for it."

"You're kidding, right?"

"It depends. Are you determined to go?"

"Yes, and if I'm rooming with the queen of control freaks, how can you expect me to do any infiltrating?"

"That's my bargain. Take it or leave it."

"Or you'll do what?" He's doing a pretty good job of staring me down.

"I'm worried about you. And if you disregard that, then what do I mean to you anyway? I'm going to be seriously pissed, just when I thought we were getting somewhere in this relationship."

"Okay, I hear you. I'll consider it, but only after I set up some house rules with Essie Sue."

"That's your problem — I'm sure you'll deal with it. And I can breathe easier because she's the most intrusive person I've ever met. There's not too much you can do that she won't keep an eye on."

"Yeah, thanks for that."

"Remember this, Ruby — none of these people is guilty of anything. The facts are now that Serena Salit had a heart attack. She could have been frightened for any number of reasons — the notebook doesn't tell us anything concrete. I just have suspicions."

"All the more reason not to be anxious about my traveling with them, honey — they're innocent, at least for now. Who knows? What I find out could ultimately be helpful. And I swear to you I won't cross the line."

"I'm holding you to that promise. And while you're at it, don't cross any train tracks, either."

19

This Canadian vacation is looking more and more unattractive to me, but now I have something besides a pleasure trip to consider. I wonder if anyone other than André knows about the affair with Serena. And if he's successfully hidden all this, what else could he be hiding? I want a good look at him this afternoon when Essie Sue entertains the latke sale committee at her house for the send-off meeting.

For once, I'm glad I promised to come early and help set up. I need more than a few words with my would-be roommate, and I'm still planning what to say as I pull into her circular driveway.

"Wipe your feet, Ruby — the gardener spilled some topsoil he was carrying onto the brickwork."

"I don't see a thing, Essie Sue," I say as I get out of the car. "I'll bet you cleaned up after him on your hands and knees."

"No, Hal did. I supervised. We decided it wasn't worth a dry-cleaning bill for what I was wearing."

"That's the royal *we* my wife is using," Hal says as he holds the front door open for me.

"What did you have on?" I ask her.

"Oh, just my blue jeans."

"But she doesn't wash her designer jeans," Hal says, "she takes them to the Harry Winston of cleaners, Precious Objects on Oak Street. Their bills have been known to exceed the retail price, so I wasn't taking any chances. What are my knees worth, compared to that?"

"You're the one who's priceless, Hal — I just hope she knows that. So why aren't you joining her for the choir adventure?"

"You mean why are you privileged to take my place? I have a golf tournament at the club and I don't want to miss it."

They lead me into the entryway, where I'm expected to wipe my feet once again on a small Oriental rug.

The objects in the Margolis home sparkle in a way I've never seen duplicated, not even in the best museums. And why not — they don't have the cleaning staff she does.

The house is much too huge for the two of them, or anyone else, for that matter. I'm always curious to see where her partygoers will tuck themselves away. People usually prefer to bunch up at parties, and since this home is so uncozy, the crowd comforts itself by hanging around the breakfast bar while ignoring the enormous baronial space in the living room. Essie Sue calls it the great room, of course — one of those pretentious real estate terms that only serves to make hapless guests feel even more alienated. I never know whether to expect wild boar roasting in the enormous fireplace or Knights Templar jousting on the faux-stone floors.

Needless to say, I can't wait for the arrival of Eternal's answer to a cult, André and company. To my surprise, he's already here, and Essie Sue has him in tow.

"You've shaved off your mustache," I blurt out as I see him. The truth is that he's changed his appearance altogether. He's swapped the Dapper Dan look for New York black, complete with shirttail hanging out and red wristband. No more shirt, tie, and jacket. I'm looking for a tattoo to complete the look, and I find it — a tiny *chai* on his pinkie finger instead of the gold ring he used to wear. Ouch — I can feel how much a tattoo on that finger must have hurt.

"The mustache was getting old," he says,

continuing his animated conversation with Essie Sue. André's never had much to say to me, now that I think of it.

"Doesn't he look stylish, Ruby?" Essie Sue says. "He's the essence of a health food store entrepreneur. Ruby's lifestyle's unhealthy, André — tell her what she should be supplementing, now that ephedra's passé."

"No, thanks — I don't supplement, Essie Sue," I say. "I never liked the idea of my bladder being richer than I am."

"That's nonsense." André shoots me a look that could tattoo my retina. "It's so nineties to think a handful of vitamins is going to harm you. I ingest twenty-five pills a day, and I'm bursting with energy."

"Bursting with something," I say. "And besides, you get yours wholesale."

"She has a point there, André," Essie Sue says. She's not coming to my rescue, she's sniffing out a possible discount, having never met a bargain she didn't pursue. "How about ten percent for friendship? After all, I appointed you choir director."

"I'm just acting director, Essie Sue. I've always told you I'm an artist, not an administrator," he says over his shoulder as he makes an escape I need to pay attention to. Anyone who can slip away from Essie Sue that skillfully gets my attention.

"I'll work on his wife, Sara," Essie Sue says. "She's over there talking to Irene Cohn."

Sara looks as happy to be conversing with Irene as I do with Essie Sue — she's perched on one of the mammoth ottomans in the great room while Irene hovers over her. Since her husband has given us the slip, I'm thinking of joining their little twosome as soon as Essie Sue's diverted by new arrivals.

I might as well have a head start on getting to know Serena's colleagues better. I also hate to begin a trip without anyone I'm close to, and these choir members aren't people I can count on as friends. Just my luck Rose isn't going along this time. She says the stay in Ohio was all the vacation she could squeeze in right now.

"Ruby — how's it going?"

Dr. Bart Goldman, Serena's ex, is blocking my path to the ottoman.

"Hi, Bart — I was just going over to talk to Irene and Sara. Want to join me?"

"I didn't know you were friendly with them." He seems surprised.

"I'm not, but I decided I'd better be if we'll be traveling together."

"Well, good luck — I find both of them

pretty standoffish. I think I'll pass."

"Hey, I definitely didn't mean to blow you off, Bart — I've known you longer than any of them. Let's go get something to drink on the patio and catch up."

We try sangria from a big pitcher on the umbrella table, and it's not bad for an Essie Sue concoction — at least, if you're not looking for the alcohol. I think she's used a twenty-to-one formula.

"Too bad she decided to go themeless," Bart says. "It's not like her. I was hoping for Canadian Club to go along with the travel topic."

I didn't remember Bart had a sense of humor — maybe he'll be fun to hang out with on the trip. We sit on a stone bench and people-watch.

"How are *you* doing?" I ask. "It must be difficult to have just finished mourning the end of your marriage and then be hit with Serena's unexpected death. Kind of a double grieving process."

"You aren't kidding — it's rough. And none of my friends even *gets* this, Ruby. You're the only person who's been able to articulate it. I feel out in limbo trying to come to grips with everything."

"I'm unfortunately well versed in the variations of grief," I say, "and it's a skill I could have done without. But I know it when I see it."

"If we drink any more of this sangria," he says, "we'll mope our way into a crying jag."

"No way we should let that happen, Bart. I'm glad you're able to get away for the trip. A change of scenery might help."

Oy. I can't get the affair between Serena and André out of my mind, and it's killing me not to have any idea if Bart knew about it. Their being lovers could have occurred after Serena's divorce or been the catalyst for it.

"There's André," I say. "Shall we call him over?"

"Sure."

There's none of the reticence Bart showed with André's wife or with Irene Cohn — maybe he's just more comfortable with another man. It's very weird, though, to think I know a secret Bart could be unaware of. But of course, André knows it all too well.

"Hey, André," I say. "How about joining us?"

He looks over at us and literally recoils. This is very odd, considering how often he must have rehearsed choir programs with Bart over the last few months as Serena's lover. I have no idea what's so different today — he should feel more comfortable with Bart, not less, now that the affair is a thing of the past. But he's definitely nervous, or down, or something.

André's obviously also feeling trapped — there's no reason *not* to talk to us, so he comes over, plastering a politician's smile on his face.

"Hi," he says to us. "I didn't ask you before, Ruby — are you excited about the trip?"

"Once I get out of town I might be. The week before a vacation is hellish — too much doubling up to do at work."

"I know what that's like. How are you, Bart? After everything, I mean."

"You mean Serena's death?" Bart says. "Still trying to work it all out in my head, not to mention my gut."

"If you need building up, drop by the store. We have lots of remedies for stress."

Strange answer, considering that Bart, AKA Dr. Goldman, knows quite a bit about remedies himself. Fortunately for him, he doesn't have to remind André of that, since Kevin suddenly backs into our little group with the subtlety of a Mack truck.

"Somebody pushed me," he says, making a feeble attempt to pick up the chips he made Bart drop on the highly polished floor. "Your wife says she's not going along on the trip, André," he adds.

"Sara's a bit undecided right now, but she'll end up joining us."

"Nope. Sara just told us she won't be there, so she and Essie Sue revised the list." Kevin turns around. "Right, Essie Sue?"

"Absolutely correct, Rabbi." Essie Sue's looming presence is always a bit jarring, and never more so than when she can catch someone off guard.

"Say hello to your new roommate, André," Essie Sue says. "You'll have to be on your best behavior with the rabbi in the next bed."

20

I'm still chuckling over Sara's coup when Kevin picks me up to go to the airport. Inviting the rabbi to move in when you can't be there is one way to make sure your philandering hubby doesn't substitute another woman's nightie for yours on the other side of the bed. I'm sure Sara goes along on most of these trips simply to keep André from adding a new conquest to his list. Not that she's been very successful at it so far. But I'd call this a very creative attempt.

I don't know who's going to have a more delightful time — me with Essie Sue, or André with Kevin. I do know which of our roommates can more easily be given the slip, though, and I'm sure André's already working on opportunities to practice his seduction techniques away from his train cabin or hotel room.

My own roommate presents a much more

difficult challenge. I went along with this because Paul obviously wants me reined in, and isn't ready to let me be a part of the investigation if I don't allay his fears about my safety. I'll live with Essie Sue because I have to, and because I don't intend to spend any time in the room other than the six or seven hours it takes to sleep. Aside from that, I'll have many opportunities to mix with other people and sniff out what's going on.

"Ruby, do you think I still have a chance with Bitsy now that I'm not rooming with her?" Kevin asks me as he weaves in and out of morning rush hour traffic.

"Depends on what kind of chance you're talking about. Last time we spoke, you were put off by her. Do you want to make a move on her or not? If so, I'm sure you'll have time to do that."

"I don't mean anything specific, Ruby. I just want to get to know her better, and to see what she's like. I don't want her to drop me before we even get started."

"Knowing Bitsy, and seeing her eye you like red meat, I don't think you need to worry that nothing will happen, Kevin. You might end up dealing with too much, not too little."

"How about you, Ruby? Essie Sue will

make you her unofficial assistant, whether you want to or not. And I'll bet she'll want to have pajama parties in the room."

"Don't worry — I'm not attending any pajama party with her that doesn't include at least three other people."

"You can't avoid talking in bed at night, or in the morning."

"I don't worry about mornings — I'm a night person, and usually so bleary-eyed when I wake up that I can't see or hear, much less talk. She can ramble on all she wants — it won't get through to me. And as for any chummy late-night conversations, I can pretend with the best of them. So in the morning I'll really sleep, and in the evening, I'll fake it."

"Are you sorry Paul's not coming along with the choir group?"

"Well, we could have fun, and maybe even do some hiking around Banff. But who knows? Maybe I'll meet some sexy Canadian when I'm up there."

"You're kidding, right? I thought you were taken."

Oy. I don't want Kevin to think I'm available to him, but on the other hand, Paul and I have no commitments, and I think I'm too young not to ever indulge my roving eye again. If not now, when? Surely not

if Paul and I do become more serious —
then it'll be too late.

"Paul's kind of my main man, Kevin, so
in that sense, I'm taken."

Hmm . . . I don't like the sound of that.
Actually, there's no way to explain my position — especially since I'm not sure what it
is myself. I'd better reroute this conversation.

"So let's get back to you, Kevin. Are you
going to try to meet any Canadian women,
or are you mostly interested in Bitsy?"

Kevin's neck seems to sink down inside
his woolen scarf. He's bundled up for
Canada in January, not late May.

"Maybe I should be like you, Ruby, and
keep my options open. There's one difference between us, though — Paul's back
home, and Bitsy's right here."

"And after you in a big way?"

"I think so."

"See where it goes. Bitsy might have her
eyes open, too."

Kevin and I take the shuttle from the
long-term parking area to the terminal —
I'd have liked to be dropped off with the
baggage and let him do the parking, but he
got nervous at all the security arrangements
and was afraid he couldn't find me. I gave
in — when Kevin's stressed, it's catching.

We go to our gate and find the usual uproar when Essie Sue's in charge. Hard to believe, but she's trying to separate us into boys' and girls' lines.

"Why?" I ask, wondering why no one else has inquired.

"It's easier to count by gender," she says, "and people are more well behaved."

"If they're in second grade," I say. "Do you see any progress here? No one's paying the least bit of attention."

"It could be worse the other way, Ruby. Help me count heads."

"Let the airline attendants do that. We can't delay the plane for latecomers, anyway."

"The rabbi's here and is going to give a short prayer for a safe trip," she yells over the chatter.

That's obviously news to Kevin, but it does stop the conversation.

He looks at me with the usual deer-in-the-headlights panic.

"How about 'bless you and keep you' — that's short and sweet," I whisper.

It's also something he knows by heart, so we get a quick benediction and Kevin earns a nod from Essie Sue.

"I owe you," he says.

I'd be a rich woman if I had a nickel for

every time I've heard that one.

I'm in a window seat beside Kevin, which is fine with me — I don't have to be on with him. I'm wondering who'll take the aisle seat, when Bitsy pops down next to him. Ha — it'd be interesting to know who she had to bribe to get hold of that prized position.

"What a surprise finding you both here," she says sweetly.

"It's a miracle," I whisper to Kevin, and then realize that he actually thinks so.

"Isn't this amazing, Ruby?" he says, apparently extremely happy to help Bitsy hold her armload of Baggies while she fastens her seat belt.

"What are all these?" I ask while she takes them back.

"Two are for my supplements to prevent jet lag, one each with baby carrots, cherry tomatoes, and diet French for dipping, and three more for mascara, liner, and blush. Plus Canadian coins that are too heavy for my wallet, and cotton pads moistened with lotion to rest my eyelids. Plus this teeny copy of the Constitution."

Kevin seems truly fascinated, while I'm only confused, not that it's any of my business.

"Uh — I thought you might have a

makeup bag for some of those," I say.

"I sent that along ahead — these are things I'll need on the plane, and they're transparent for the inspectors. I like to be prepared for everything, although they confiscated my fingernail scissors. I'd been told that if they weren't hidden, you could take them on board."

I don't dare ask who told her that one, or more important, why she included the last Baggie. But Kevin does.

"Why that?" he says, pointing at the Baggie containing the Constitution.

"When you're traveling out of the country, who knows when you'll need a copy?" she says. "It could save you from being thrown in jail or something."

I consider reminding her that outside our borders the book means nothing, but I let it go.

"I hear Barbara Jordan always did that," Kevin says. "See, Ruby?" He gives me a nudge with his elbow. I think he's trying to tell me she's just moved up a notch on the worthiness scale.

I decide on the spot to give these two a chance to dip some baby carrots together, so I propel myself across their laps and take a walk down the aisle for a bathroom break before the beverage cart blocks the way.

Irene is happily ensconced in a two-seater next to André, with no sign of his wife, Sara, who must not have changed her mind. Essie Sue's also in the aisle, keeping several choir members from reading their paperbacks.

"I'm just energizing the group," she tells me. "Maybe I'll go back and talk to the rabbi."

"He's engrossed in conversation with Bitsy," I say. "Give them a chance to talk, Essie Sue."

"I thought that might be a good match," she says, "but now I'm not so sure. Who knows if she's prepared to be a clergy wife?"

"Who ever is?" I say. "And it's beside the point — let him have a little fun. Why does everyone have to be a potential spouse?"

"Because he's a rabbi, Ruby — you know that. They can't fool around."

"But he gets to date someone without marrying them, right?"

"Okay, I'll leave them alone. But you're responsible to see that they don't go too far."

"I have to go to the bathroom now."

I wouldn't give Essie Sue the satisfaction, but I'm leery of little Bitsy, too. That gleam in her eye is a bit too steely for me. But that doesn't mean Kevin needs tracking like a teenager.

I'm waiting at the bathroom door when Bart Goldman comes out and almost slams into me. He takes a step back when he sees me.

"I didn't mean to surprise you," I say. "You look shocked."

"No, no — I'm okay. I mean, I'm just a little spaced out from the trip."

None of what he says makes much sense — especially since the trip's hardly started. But one thing's for sure — Bart's definitely groggy. Wonder what he's on?

21

I crawl back to my window seat, with no help whatsoever from Kevin and Bitsy, who won't even bend their knees sideways to let me pass. I get my revenge, though, when I have to step on their feet in order to wedge my body through. My big hurry is to make sure that I won't miss flying over the snow-topped Mount Ranier on our way to the Seattle-Tacoma airport. I'm barely seated when there it is, peeking out of the clouds like a giant iced doughnut gleaming in the sunlight. I poke at Kevin so that he and Bitsy can see, but their conversation takes precedence.

I've never understood how the flying public could possibly be so blasé about soaring thirty thousand feet above the earth. Forget that my generation's been airborne since childhood — familiarity's no excuse for sticking your nose in a book and ignoring a cotton-cloud carpet stretching beneath you for miles, or the course of a river cutting a state in half, or starlike city lights making it seem as if the plane's flying upside down.

"Can you believe how Ranier is suddenly just *there?*" I say.

"I hope I get my kosher meal," Bitsy answers. "If you're not paying attention, someone else grabs it."

So she *is* paying attention to something.

"I didn't know you kept kosher," Kevin says.

"I don't. My travel agent put me on to it. You get fewer carbs with a kosher meal — they give you a lot of brisket instead of the Mexicali Enchiladas. You should try it, Rabbi."

Odd, but in Bitsy-world it seems perfectly plausible to explain to the rabbi why he should get a kosher plate. Mine is not to reason why, but they've missed Mount Ranier and we're now circling Sea-Tac, so I'm pretty sure this means the kosher meal is out.

We do get fed, for some reason, on the short flight from Seattle to Vancouver. We're treated to a bistro bag containing a dry turkey sandwich and a bottle of water. The flight attendant is also passing around bags of baked chips made specially for the airline.

149

Fortunately, the chips on planes are unknown in real life — they exist only in a rarified atmosphere. Even if I wanted mine, I don't get the chance.

"People, do not eat those chips."

Essie Sue is following the attendant down the aisle, gathering the bags from our collective laps as quickly as they're given to us.

"We need the chips for our cocktail party on the train," she says, forcing us to toss our goodies into a large brown paper Kroger bag. "Remember, we were unable to raise the funds for this choir trip, and most of you are having to subsidize our efforts."

Not subsidize — *pay for.* And now she can't even throw us a complimentary party.

"Anyone purchasing those convenient little alcoholic beverages is asked to either save them or to buy an extra bottle for our event. It's all for a good cause."

The flight attendant is being a pretty good sport about this — either that, or she's already been intimidated. She does draw the line, however, when Essie Sue tries to collect from the other passengers. Luckily, we're about to land, and we're all called to our seats.

The Vancouver airport at uninhabited Sea Island looks like a piece of the planet Mars — it exists only as a receptacle for planes. It is, though, the only uninteresting bit of scenery in the entire vicinity. To me, Vancouver is a marvel of the universe, a jewel of a city where beaches and mountains are within walking distance of the world's most diverse and cosmopolitan population. I adore the place, and I'm just sorry we're only using it as a stopover.

When we arrive at our hotel in downtown Vancouver, I'm so glad to stretch my legs and get away from Kevin's and Bitsy's idea of flirtatious banter that I forget the ordeal to come. Not for long, though — Essie Sue has already registered for our double room and wrangled an upgrade as the group leader. I don't remember anyone electing her group leader, but I'm not about to complain when I hear we're in a one-bedroom suite.

"I'll take the living room," I say.

"Don't be silly, Ruby — you certainly don't want to give up one of our two queen-size beds for a pullout sofa in the living room, do you?"

"Uh-huh. Sure do."

"I'm sure I'll be scheduling important meetings in the living room — after all, that's why I needed the upgrade."

"I can sleep through meetings," I say. "No problem."

She's not kidding — after an unbelievable dinner of broiled halibut in a restaurant next door to the hotel, she's buttonholed me, Kevin, Bitsy, and André for a "strategy" meeting in our suite.

I've had quite enough of Kevin and Bitsy for one day, and I obviously can't get away from my roomie, but I am curious about André Korman. The rest of us are pretty droopy, but the only way I can describe him is that he looks as if he were a woman who just put on fresh makeup. That's as far as the analogy goes, but it's accurate — this is a guy who's always on. It's apparent that he's flattered to be included, which already says a lot about him, in my opinion.

As for me, I'm angling for a quick getaway after a brief period of polite hostessing at the strategy meeting, so I guess I won't have much time to observe André — there'll be other opportunities. Some of us are getting together in an hour for a long walk along Hornby Street, and I don't want to miss that.

"Remember, Essie Sue, I only have an hour for this meeting," I say while we're serving our guests diet sodas from the mini-bar. "I know how your get-togethers can expand."

"Fine, Ruby, although I don't know why

you're so anxious to sightsee tonight. We have plenty of gorgeous scenery to enjoy on the train trip through the Rockies."

"Just because," I say. I don't intend to waste my energy dragging out every discussion with her. Although I'm biting my tongue as I watch her divide each can into two servings.

"We have to conserve, people," she announces to Kevin, Bitsy, and André. "I haven't had a chance to get to a grocery store yet, and these minibar refreshments are expensive."

"Skip mine," I say. "I'm going out later."

"I already skipped yours, Ruby," she says. "This way there'll only be four of us sharing the two cans."

Why do I bother?

Kevin drinks his glass in one gulp. "Okay, Essie Sue, what do we have to talk about?" he says. He seems emboldened with Bitsy at his side, and I'm thinking maybe I'm not the only one who has plans.

Essie Sue's about to answer Kevin, when André upstages her.

"I'm surprised at you, Rabbi," he says. "Since Essie Sue has been kind enough to come along on the trip to help organize us, it's only natural that she'd have lots of strategy to discuss. We should give her our respect."

Whoa — this guy's just pulled off a triple-header. He's managed to make Kevin look bad, flatter Essie Sue, and give lip service to the respect she never gets, all in one swoop. I think I've observed all I need to.

"Why, aren't you sweet," she says. "How nice to be appreciated for a change, and from a most unlikely source."

Ha — nobody gets a real break with Essie Sue, but André chooses not to notice the small slur amid the faint praise. He manages a look of modest adoration. Yep, he's a player.

Just as the atmosphere is getting a bit too honeyed for my taste, my cell phone rings. I look to see that it's Paul calling. Goody — a call I've wanted, *plus* an excuse to go in the other room.

Essie Sue's way ahead of me.

"Take your call later, Ruby. This is important, and you're leaving early, besides."

"Excuse me, everyone, I'm going in the other room to take this," I say.

"But that's my bedroom," Essie Sue says. "You're sleeping here in the living room, remember?"

"So are you taking them all into your room?" I say, directing a fast "Hi, hold on" into the phone. "Tell me quick, Essie Sue, so I'll know where to go for the phone call."

"Go," she says, waving her hand toward the bedroom.

There's a chair in her bedroom, and it's far away from the door, so I take that for maximum privacy. Besides, I don't dare jump on her bed — too much fallout even for me to handle.

"Hi, babe," I say, "sorry for the wait. I'm so glad you called."

"Me, too," Paul says. "How was the flight?"

"I sat by Kevin and Bitsy," I tell him. "That should say it all."

"My sympathy. Will you be in twin beds with Essie Sue tonight?"

"No, I'm sleeping on the pullout in the living room — we'll be up close and personal on the train far too much as it is. Hey, I miss you. But your call is getting me out of a meeting here in the suite. I'm holed up in Essie Sue's bedroom while she's boring — uh, entertaining — André, Kevin, and Bitsy."

"They're all in the living room?"

"Yeah. Why?"

"Can you talk, honey?"

"Of course. I'm talking now, right? If you mean how private is this, I think it's okay. I'm sitting across the room away from the living area, and I can see the door from here, so no one can surprise me. Don't *you* be surprised, though, if Essie Sue pops in here every five minutes to get me off the phone."

"Ruby, try to keep your voice low, and mostly listen — which means I'll do the talking, okay?"

"Sure. What's the matter? Are you all right?"

"I'm fine except for not liking it that you're in another country."

"A friendly one, though. And adjacent."

"Ha."

"Okay, not funny," I say. "What's up?"

"Right after you flew out of here, I got a call from Serena's sister, Joellyn, in Ohio. Serena's body was reexamined and the lab results just came in. She didn't die of a heart attack."

"You're kidding. Really? So Joellyn's ESP was right on, huh?"

"Dead on, excuse the pun."

"What was — uh-oh — hold on," I say.

If you can slam open a door in the same way you can slam it shut, then Essie Sue does it. I'm glad I warned Paul.

"Ruby, I know you're talking to that policeman — he's the only one who'd keep you this long."

"Believe it or not, I have quite a few other friends who're capable of burning up the wires," I say. "Do I have to give you a list of my incoming calls just because we're rooming together?"

"But we need you in the meeting."

"I'll be there as soon as I can."

"Well, you're not leaving here for that walk with the others," she says. "You owe me some time."

"We'll discuss it later," I say, realizing that she's already yelled out that I'm talking to the policeman.

"Come on, Ruby."

"Out, Essie Sue. And close the door."

"She just flounced out," I tell Paul. "I guess you heard that she told everyone it was you on the phone."

"Yeah, but you didn't confirm it. Good thinking."

"I should have waited to take this call when I was out on my walk later," I say. "It's just that I wanted to talk to you."

"You didn't know the nature of the call, hon. Don't worry about it. No one heard us."

"Thank goodness for cells — I'd never trust her not to pick up the extension if you'd called the room."

"This can wait an hour," Paul says, "but I

157

wanted you to know ASAP. Besides, how do you know you'll have privacy stepping away from a group of people?"

"I don't, except for the fact that those people don't include Essie Sue. Or André, Kevin, or Bitsy, for that matter. But you're not stopping now."

"No, not with your curiosity," he says. "You'd never let me get away with it."

"So what killed her?" I whisper.

"It hasn't been identified yet. But they found a toxic substance in the body, even though it certainly wasn't apparent at first."

"How could someone have poisoned her with so many people around?" I say.

"Well, she probably ate something — all of you were trying out those latkes, right? And she was backstage for a few minutes before the performance. There were op-portunities — we just don't know how it was done yet."

"Wow. I'm still floored. Rose must be plotzing. Not to mention Joellyn. Did either of them have any idea what might have hap-pened, or when it happened?"

"No. Joellyn just learned about it a few hours ago, and she called Rose, and then me."

"Did you talk to Rose?"

"No, she wasn't home. Joellyn said they

were both upset, of course — this was something they'd dreaded ever since Joellyn decided to have the body exhumed."

"What will you do now?"

"Talk to everyone again in light of what's happened, and hold tight to see what substance is identified."

"I'm assuming you don't want anyone here to know yet," I say.

"True — I don't want you saying anything, for your own safety as well as for other considerations. But I'm not so sure we'll have the luxury of keeping this information confidential. I have no idea if Rose has called anyone there, and Bart keeps in touch with Joellyn — he might have already emailed her from the road. My guess is that people do know about this procedure. And once I start reinterviewing, it's not going to be a secret for long. The papers'll get it, too."

"So what should I do if someone asks me?"

"I'd feign ignorance. They have no way of knowing what I've told you."

"They'll know."

"So what? Pretend you don't know and you won't have to discuss it."

"It'll be interesting, though, to see who does hear about it here."

"Ruby, there's something I haven't said."

"Will I like it?"

"No. I want you to come home. Think of some excuse."

"Don't be silly — I'm in no danger."

"If someone involved decides you might be watching or listening on my behalf, it won't be safe for you."

"You mean spying? Why can't I do that? It's the perfect time, since you can't be here. And everyone knows I'm a snoop — they'll expect it of me."

"We're in the early stages of this investigation, Ruby, and I don't even know what we're dealing with. I want you home."

"Essie Sue's coming in again," I say. "And I think my battery's running out, too. I'll get back to you later."

Talk about self-sabotage. I didn't even get to hear any sweet nothings from my sweetie. But hey, I had no choice. No way am I leaving now.

22

Before I go back into the living area I make a quick call to my friend Elizabeth's room. She's the one who organized the after-dinner walk tonight.

No answer — I *knew* this would happen. We planned to meet in the lobby and take along anyone who showed up — it's easier not to have to keep up with people. Since they all know I'm rooming with Essie Sue, I guess they figured I got stuck. Or worse, that she'd show up down in the lobby with me. I don't blame them for not waiting. I know I could take off and try to catch up with them, but it's been a while, and they could be blocks away by now.

It was worth skipping the walk to talk to Paul — I miss him. But certainly not enough to go home. He should know me better than that by now. This trip has been planned for months, so I have the perfect excuse to be present, and no one could suspect I'm here for any other purpose than to attend the ChoirFest. What more could I want than to have most of the choir here? People are usually relaxed on a trip, and conversations can flow easily. I'm certainly going to be Miss Congeniality if it'll help get information.

The thought of it is killing me, but I think my best bet is to go back and be a part of the meeting. If Kevin and Bitsy decide to go off by themselves, it'll be a good idea to talk to André with Essie Sue as a buffer. Maybe he'll be so busy impressing *her* that he won't notice I'm paying attention.

Essie Sue opens the bedroom door again and makes things easy for me.

"Ruby, where are you? You promised to meet with us, and now you're taking advantage of my good nature."

"You're absolutely right," I say. "I'm really sorry, folks — I didn't know I'd be on the phone so long. Since I haven't been part of the meeting at all, I'll stay here instead of joining the group downstairs."

Kevin gives me a quick look. If he knew how to raise an eyebrow, I'm sure this would be the time to do it, but that's not part of his repertoire. Fortunately, he's the only one in the group who knows me well enough to question my giving up a good time for an idiotic meeting. I owe him one for not blurting out anything.

André pats the seat beside him on the sofa, and I accept.

"Thanks," I say, smiling in the grateful way he'd expect from any woman who's the recipient of his generosity.

My response hits its mark. "You know, Ruby," he says, "you and I don't know each other very well. We should do something about that."

I give another grateful smile. Wish I could blush, but I'm as helpless at that as Kevin is with an eyebrow raise. Fortunately, André's the type of guy who automatically fills in the blanks in his favor.

"I understand you're responsible for organizing the Eternal contingent here," I say. "Good job."

I think I'll stop after this — this man's wife isn't here, and he's notorious for hitting on anything that moves. That's not the way I want to extract any goodies from him.

"Okay, you two — make your small talk later," Essie Sue says, seeming not altogether displeased. Since I'm sure she's not interested in fixing me up with a married man, I can only surmise she's just relieved at my sudden compliance tonight.

"We're planning for our hospitality when we meet the other choir organizations," she says. "Everyone thought my plan for a cocktail party on the tour train would be fun."

Ha — no naysayers in this crowd; I'm sure she can get whatever she wants.

"We board in the morning," she says, "so the event could take place halfway through the afternoon. I'm counting on each of you to be a cohost."

"What are we serving besides the drinks and snacks you confiscated from the plane?" I ask. "We'll have to hit a grocery store before we board the train, and that's not always easy in the middle of downtown."

"This was all discussed while you were on the phone, Ruby," Essie Sue says.

"Yeah, who was that you were talking to?" Kevin asks.

He would.

"A couple of people, actually," I say. "Just answering messages and checking in to let people know I'd arrived. I do have business commitments back home."

"But which one called you?" Bitsy says. "Was it the policeman?"

I ignore that, but she's not deterred. "Ruby's been going out with a policeman," she explains to André.

He raises both eyebrows — a move that's definitely in *his* repertoire if not in Kevin's.

"A little bit of gossip I'd not heard," he says.

Yuck. Although maybe it'll keep me off his hit list.

"Which policeman?" André says.

"Lieutenant Paul Lundy. I've known him for years." Essie Sue can't stand losing control of the conversation for more than a minute, so I'm not surprised she's plunged in.

"I know him, too," André says. "He's the one who questioned some of us the day Serena had the heart attack."

"Thank goodness they didn't take our prints," Bitsy says. "I was fingerprinted once and they made me cut two of my beautiful long nails — they kept sliding on the ink. Can you believe it?"

"They must have been awfully long," I say, grabbing on to any trivia I can to keep the focus off Paul and me. If André knows about any suspicions of murder, he's certainly not showing it — he's being a regular Mr. Casual. But if I thought he was diverted, I was wrong.

"So, Ruby," André says, "is your relationship with Lieutenant Lundy serious?"

"I'm not serious about anyone," I say, immediately making myself fair game again, I guess.

"Well, I thought it was serious," Kevin

says. "He's the only one you've been seeing since you broke up with Ed Levinger."

I can see André's face going into questioning mode already.

"Hey, Essie Sue," I say, "I thought this was supposed to be such an important meeting. Am I the subject, or do you have other things to deliberate?"

"You're right, Ruby," Essie Sue says, "but we still want to know if it was Paul who called you. If so, then he sounds like a boyfriend to me."

"Okay, I'm dating him and he called," I say. Better to give in on that point than to let them know the call was professional — at least in part. "I'm assuming I'm not required to report our conversation," I say, "and don't you think this is getting a bit intrusive even for you, Essie Sue?"

Never one to apologize, she gives me a nod. "Back to business," she says. "I want our group to wear name tags so that the other choirs can know us immediately. I have the blanks here," she says as she dumps a bagful on the coffee table for us to fill out.

It takes about fifteen minutes for me to do my share, and then I figure the others might be back from their walk and wandering around in the lobby. I'll try to talk to André on the train tomorrow — Bitsy and

Kevin don't seem to be leaving, and I could be stuck here all night if I don't make my move now.

"Bye, all," I say, heading for the door, "have to meet some people."

"But we have more to do," Essie Sue says, "and after that I thought you and I could watch TV in our pajamas like I do with Hal."

"Why don't you call him?" I suggest as I leave. Playing Hal to Essie Sue is not my idea of fun on my only night in Vancouver. Maybe she'll be asleep by the time I get back.

23

I see Bart Goldman as I get off the elevator.

"Are you heading upstairs?" I say.

"Yeah. I thought you were going on the walk with us," he says.

"It's a long story," I say. "Where are the others?"

"Most of them were tired and already went up to their rooms. I was thinking of doing something, but most of these people in the lobby are strangers to me."

"Doesn't say much for the party spirit in our group, does it? Let's have a drink on our own," I say.

"Okay, how about one of these sofas right here? You don't even have to go into the cocktail lounge."

"You know, Bart, I hate sticking to the hotel. Let's at least go across the street. I saw lots of places over there this afternoon."

My main worry is that Essie Sue will come down here looking for me, so I hurry us out the revolving doors to safety. Besides, I really do prefer finding nightspots outside the hotel. Dr. Bart Goldman might not be my choice to roam the town with, but we can at least explore something other than the lobby for our drink.

There is indeed a nice pubby place up the block, complete with a French Canadian chanteuse at the piano. To me, any love song in French is ten times more erotic than one in English, regardless of how good the singer is. This one isn't bad at all. And I can see what's up with Bart while I'm at it. Paul would be proud of me — once he got over my listening to love songs over drinks with another man. But come on — it's only Bart. Although we do order some very dusky cognac together.

After I indulge myself for a few minutes pretending Bart is Paul, I get the guilts and try to make conversation.

"How're you doing?" I ask. "I guess this is your first trip in a while."

"Yeah, first since Serena and I divorced, as a matter of fact. I just hadn't felt like going anywhere, and then after she died, I had even less energy for it."

I want to ask if he's been in touch with her sister, but I hold off. Although we really don't have that much in common other than

Serena, so I figure he'll get around to it himself if I'm patient. Of course, I'm not even convinced of the cliché that patience is a virtue, and if it is, it's certainly not my virtue.

"Have you thought about dating yet?" I say, and then am instantly sorry. He's going to think *I'm* interested, when I'm really just fishing for conversation. Bart's one of those guys who's not objectionable, but that's the sexiest thing you can say about him. Though I understand he's a busy doctor, his energy level when it comes to anything else has always seemed to me about a zero. And the energy's where it's at in the mating dance, at least in my not-so-humble opinion. It certainly outplays looks, or even personality. No energy, no spark — and I don't mean nervous energy or hyperactivity, but whatever it is the Energizer Bunny has that makes him a proliferating rabbit and not lox. It comes from the core, and if they don't have it, they ain't gonna get it.

"Yes, I've thought a lot about dating," he says in answer to my question. "But it's not so easy in a place like Eternal."

"If you were a woman, I'd agree with you," I say, "but a male on this planet who happens to have a successful medical practice? Don't tell me the girls weren't on your

170

trail the minute they heard about your divorce last year."

"A few were, but they all seemed the same — it's hard to describe them."

"You mean the casserole crowd?" I say. "They *are* kind of interchangeable."

"Yeah, they were at my door at first, but I guess I didn't respond well when people tried to fix me up."

I can sympathize there. "I know what you mean," I say. "The time you're half in shock and least ready to show your best side is the very moment your friends are most interested in shining a light on you. Then, after three or four months, they don't try so hard."

"I was relieved when they quit trying, Ruby. I figured I'd rather get dates on my own. Less pressure."

I can relate, but at the same time, he does sound insecure. Still, the matchmaker in me hopes he doesn't give up. Not everyone's looking for what I'm looking for, and he's a nice guy. Oy — as I say the words *nice guy* to myself, I'm articulating half the problem. On the other hand, my practical side would never underestimate the face value of a nice Jewish doctor whose worst fault is that he's just okay.

"How about you, Ruby? I know you date,

but you're not going steady, are you?"

His vocabulary needs an upgrade, but we're part of the same operating system, so I get it.

"I wouldn't say I'm going steady, Bart, but I am seeing someone."

"Does that mean you'd go out with me if we hit it off? You're so easy to talk to, and I feel you understand me."

All too well, and now we're back to the square one I thought I was avoiding.

"I don't think I'm a good bet right now, Bart, but I have paid my dues, and I do understand you. It's not easy to replace someone you've been with for a long time."

I remember that this is a dual-purpose get-together, so I nudge the subject back to Serena.

"Do you think about Serena a lot, or are you just feeling in limbo?" I ask.

He looks uneasy. "I find myself playing what-if," he says.

"That's natural. Do you have anyone to talk to when you get in a funk?"

At first he's quiet, but then says, "I email Joellyn quite a bit."

"Is that helpful?"

"Well, she used to be reticent right after the divorce, since of course she sided with Serena. But now that Serena's gone, we've

172

grown closer."

"Do you phone her, too? I'm thinking of like now, when it's inconvenient to drag a laptop around."

Gotta go easy here — this is obviously none of my business.

"Vancouver has plenty of Internet cafés," he says. "I guess on the road, though, it might be a different matter. And in answer to your question, we mostly email."

I'm dying to ask if there's any news, but I don't dare, and he's not going that way so far.

"How about Rose?" I say. "She visited Joellyn, so I thought maybe that friendship might have brought you two closer together, too."

"Rose took Serena's side completely," he says. "I don't think she's that good for Joellyn — she's not letting her get over her sister's death."

I give him time to say more — I don't want to blow this by asking for specifics. While I wait, the singer is belting out some Josephine Baker, and I'm loving it. But since I'm here by my lonely, it's not going to do me any good. I could tell Paul about it later, but frankly, it's more Ed's thing than his, and that's over. It's obviously off Bart's radar completely — she might as well be calling *sooooie* as crooning a love song.

"I guess Rose is grieving, too," I say, mostly making conversation, but he takes it the wrong way.

"I forgot you're a good friend of Rose's," he says. "I just don't see the point of that trip to Ohio."

Maybe he's just feeling left out that Joellyn didn't ask him to visit.

"I haven't seen a lot of Rose lately," I say. "I've been busy trying to get out of town."

"Wonder why Rose didn't come, too," he says. "She is in the choir."

"I think it was the trip to Ohio — too much travel in a short space of time."

"Another reason she shouldn't have gone there," he says, gulping instead of sipping his current cognac.

Methinks he's making too much of this, and I wonder why he cares one way or the other. And it's certainly interesting that we're both avoiding any mention of the discoveries Rose made in Ohio. He has to know, if he's emailing Joellyn all the time. Unless he's not in the loop. And if not, why not? I'd love to find out whether Bart's keeping secrets from me or they're keeping secrets from him.

24

I get back to our hotel corridor around eleven, hopefully after Essie Sue's bedtime. My real fantasy is to stay out all night and be totally safe from any pillow talk, but that isn't exactly practical — and certainly not with Bart. I slide my key card silently into the slot and hope the heavy door doesn't make any noise. It doesn't open. I try three more times. Nothing. This isn't the first time I've had a key card that was either mis-programmed or not programmed at all.

I go back down to the lobby despite the fact that I'm experiencing a sudden letdown from the long flight and the nonstop activity tonight, but what choice do I have? And maybe the cognac is playing its part, too. I persuade the bellman to come up with me so he can do some of the legwork if the door still doesn't open. A new card would be ideal, but of course that's not the way it works. First, the guest must always be subjected to instruction as to how to put the card in the slot.

"Upside down with the stripe to the right," the desk clerk reminds me downstairs. "It's really very simple."

He would have made a great kindergarten teacher.

"I did that," I say, earning a look reserved for the legions of dummies who nightly torture the wise ones at the front desk.

"Did you knock?" he adds.

"No, my roommate's asleep by now," I say.

When I'm finally granted leave to bring the bellman to my floor, I realize I'll have to pay for it two ways. Besides the obvious one, he's also noisier than I am. By the third door rattle, I hear Essie Sue yelling from her bed.

"Is that you, Ruby?"

"Sorry, Essie Sue."

"I double-bolted the door," she says. "You can't be too careful."

I'm embarrassed to look at the bellman, who, since he's waiting for my tip, has to hold in his condescension. I guess I *am* dumber than they are.

When I finally get inside the room, I don't have the energy to show my annoyance, aside from asking if she could promise not to bolt the door from now on.

"I wouldn't have to go through this if you didn't stay out so late, Ruby," she says, tying the sash on her three-piece Japanese pajama outfit in jade green satin. "Someone said they saw you in the lobby with Bart Goldman. You aren't thinking of dating him, are you? It would only be on the rebound. He's not over Serena yet."

"We had a drink," I say. "And I'm falling asleep on my feet. Just point me toward the sofa bed."

"But you haven't unpacked yet."

"I'm not unpacking — we leave tomorrow. Hopefully, my flannel PJs aren't too far down in the suitcase."

"I looked at the sofa, and I don't think there are any sheets on it," she says. "They might be in the linen closet with the extra blankets."

I'm so tired I'm ready to cry at this point.

"You can sleep in my room," she says, "in the other bed."

"I'll just flop on the bare sofa."

"There's no way you're sleeping without sheets," she says, taking my hand and leading me to the bedroom. "I have a surprise for you — I found your pajamas for you and laid them out on the bed. Even though you could have dressed up a bit more for the trip — don't you have travel sleepwear?"

All I can manage to mutter is, "Flannel's good for Canada." And I'm doubly thrilled that she went through my suitcase — that, I can't deal with at all in my present stupor. I wash up in the bathroom and literally fall into bed. At this point, I'd sleep with an ax murderer if his bed was as soft as this one is.

I do notice that the lights don't go off, and the TV goes on.

"This is what I've been looking forward to," she says, waving the remote at me, "our pajama party. Hal doesn't like the same shows I do. Let's watch 'Today's Special Value' on QVC — can you imagine that they have this in Canada, too?"

I burrow under the covers.

"I think I should call in for this," she says. "Help me decide."

I feel a tinkle in my ear.

"I poured you half of my Diet Coke," she says, "with ice. It's refreshing."

I'm not sure, but I think she and her remote have moved over to my bed — somewhere near my head.

"Look, Ruby." She's plumping up my pillows and settling in. "This is a knitting machine they're showing on the screen. You weave the yarn in and out of these steel dividers — it's a lot quicker than using knitting needles. I can use it in bed at night. Hurry up before they put something else on — should I buy this?"

"It's probably a taped show in Canada," I say from under my blanket.

"No, it's not."

"Okay, buy it."

"Not until you see it." She turns me over, puts one of the pillows behind my neck, and feeds me a sip of Diet Coke.

"Look at the item. Quick."

Maybe she'll buy it and go to bed. And since I've already opened my mouth, it's not much of a stretch to open my eyes, too.

"Essie Sue, this knitting machine is a three-foot long wooden stick with nails in it. If you maneuver this into bed with you, you could put Hal's eyes out."

"It comes with an instructional video. At fifty-eight dollars, it's a steal. At the end of the day it goes back to its regular price of sixty-eight dollars."

"If you buy it, will you go to sleep? We have an all-day train trip tomorrow."

I warn her not to call from the hotel phone, and it takes thirty minutes to get an 800 number that doesn't produce a busy signal from the switchboard.

"I got through," she says, nudging my

elbow in case I'm not thoroughly awake. "But they're not recognizing my account because I'm not calling from my home phone, and I forgot my password. I need to hang up and call Hal in Texas. I have it written down in a big list on the refrigerator with all my passwords and account numbers."

"Please don't call Hal — it's three in the morning there." Now, of course, I'm thoroughly awake.

Through the indomitable efforts of customer service not to lose a sale, we reach a resolution after she finally finds her credit card.

By now I've had a glass of Diet Coke with caffeine, and we move on to a French Canadian station.

"Just to practice the language," she says, and frankly, anything's better than another shopping struggle.

"Isn't this fun, Ruby?" she says. "I knew we'd love this girl time. But all this French is making me sleepy, so I'm going back to my bed."

The room's finally dark, she snores through her eye mask, her noseguard, and her retainer, and I'm left counting loops of yarn crisscrossing sixty-five rows of nails, in French.

25

I think I slept about an hour — my mind's on the six o'clock wake-up call to meet in the lobby at seven. Essie Sue's still asleep, and I'm not about to wake her with the sound of the shower. I wobble barefoot into the living room — the clock in here says five. Thankfully, my suitcase is in this room, too, hardly disturbed from last night. My favorite dark wine sweater's on top, with a comfortable pair of jeans. I change clothes, use the second bathroom to wash in the sink, and I'm out the door. There's no way I can take her company first thing in the morning, and it's worth anything to make an early exit. I'll have two hours without having to make conversation.

I'm standing by the elevator, glancing idly down one of the corridors, when I see André letting himself into one of the rooms. Wonder where he's been all night? And was his rabbinical roommate out with him, too?

I'm alone in the elevator, as I expected, and no one gets on before the stop in the lobby.

"Ruby, what are you doing here?" It's Kevin, standing right where the door opens to let me out.

"Well, I can certainly ask the same," I say. "You and I aren't exactly morning people."

"Don't forget," he says, "that it's later than this in Eternal."

"I did forget that, but the time change doesn't mean that I got any more sleep last night."

"Did Essie Sue keep you up?"

"That's the least of it," I say. "I just wanted out of there this morning."

Kevin's wearing a gray sweater and his tartan wool scarf — I think the plaid must look Canadian to him. He has his suitcase, too.

"What happened with you last night?" I say.

"Like what?"

I'm not quite ready to say I saw André this morning — I'd rather have Kevin spill a few things first. For all I know, he invited Bitsy to his room and asked André to sleep somewhere else. That's a reach, though.

"Did you and Bitsy go out on the town after the meeting?"

"Well, Bitsy wanted to come back to my room after, to share a fruit platter from room service, but I didn't know what André was going to do, so I didn't think it was a good idea. We turned in early."

"Why didn't you work it out with him?" I say.

"Huh?"

"Guys do these things, Kevin. He'd understand."

"It was too much planning for me," he says.

"Are you still a little bit afraid of Bitsy?" I ask.

"She's kind of unpredictable," he says. "I'd rather just start by taking her out to dinner in Eternal."

"But you thought you might be rooming with her at one point."

"That was more or less a fantasy," he says.

"How about taking her out to dinner here?" I say. "Even if you don't want to room-hop right now, there are times when you can't let a good opportunity go by."

"I'm hungry," he says, blatantly changing the subject. "Let's see if the coffee shop is open."

"Yeah, I need my coffee and a copy of the Vancouver paper," I say.

There's a lone waitress setting up in the

coffee shop, and the sign says they're not open until six.

"There's a machine near the side entrance," she tells us, "and they have bottles of Frappuccino."

"Cold coffee?" Kevin says.

"It has caffeine in it," I say. "Let's go for it."

We grab comfortable chairs in a room adjoining the lobby — I'd rather be out of Essie Sue's notice for as long as possible. No newspapers in sight yet, so I take this chance to get more out of Kevin.

"How was André as a sleep-mate?" I say. "Did he talk you to death like Essie Sue did me?"

"Uh, to tell you the truth, Ruby, he hadn't come in yet when I went to sleep last night, and this morning, he must have gone for a jog or something before I got up. His suitcase was still there, but he wasn't."

"So you didn't see him at all last night?"

"Nope."

For Kevin's sake, I hope André didn't connect with Bitsy. Somehow, though, I don't think she'd be interested in a married man. My guess is she has very specific marriage plans of her own, and that they don't include being anyone's mistress first.

I wish Kevin knew more about the latest

Serena developments, but I'm afraid to tell him. Since he's such a fixture with our Temple Rita group, he'd be an extra pair of eyes for me and Paul, and wouldn't be likely to be noticed. But he doesn't even know what a poker face *is,* making him totally unreliable undercover. I can just see him giving something away to André or Bitsy, even without meaning to.

It's six, and we both race for the coffee shop. Kevin orders a full breakfast, and I'm happy to get an English muffin and some hot coffee.

"Can I get grits with my eggs?" he asks the waitress. She's clueless.

"Not here," I say. "She doesn't even know what you're talking about."

"We have reindeer jerky," she says. "Out-of-towners like that."

"Just the eggs, then," he says. "And Texas toast."

"Hotel toast," I tell her. "Like mine."

"What are you two doing here so early?" It's Bitsy, followed by half the choir, or at least all those who responded to the wake-up call. "You look awfully cozy."

"We're not cozy," Kevin says. "It's just Ruby."

His attempt to save the day goes down cold with Bitsy, who continues to glare at

185

me. This time, I don't even bother to help him explain — I'm too tired from my all-nighter.

I can see that André's avoiding our table — he's headed to one in the corner with his quartet-mates Irene and Bart, plus a perky newcomer from one of the Canadian choirs who'll be joining us on the train trip.

I'm barely conscious of Kevin's and Bitsy's prattle, just happy to refuel with the coffee and forget that I got no sleep last night. My wake-up ritual would be even better with a newspaper to read, but no luck there.

"Roundup time, people — let's start filling up those buses to the railroad station. As you go through the lobby, bring along any of our group who've strayed from the fold."

Well, at least I managed to avoid Essie Sue for an hour, if not two. She's happily on the rampage, with easy prey so early in the morning — we're all groggy from the plane trip and last night's exploration of the city. I try to get to the lobby ahead of her, but she catches up with me.

"Why didn't you wake me, Ruby? We could have talked over coffee in bed, or watched one of the early morning shows."

I shudder to think what she might have

186

purchased at five in the morning — Irish sweaters for winters in the Sunbelt? Or maybe they feature clearance items at that hour. I run for one of the buses while she's still busy herding.

Too bad it's such a short trip from the hotel to the railroad station — the bus I've chosen is full of strangers, who're refreshingly different from my hometown crowd. This group is from Washington State — crossing the border into British Columbia is an ordinary occurrence for them.

"Have you made this trip before?" I ask the very cute guy sitting next to me, who has that unusual combination of jet black hair and blue eyes I've always found fascinating. He's in jeans, wearing a brown leather jacket over a heathery blue sweater that just happens to be the color of his eyes, and his boots could have easily come from one of the boot makers in downtown Austin. I tell him that before he can answer my first question.

"Who are you?" he says with a smile that makes me glad I spoke up.

"So which shall we answer," I say, "your one question or my two?"

"No, your *three,*" he says. "You just asked another, so I'd better try keeping up with you. I've never made this particular train

187

trip before, but I've been to all these destinations many times — Vancouver, Banff, and Lake Louise. And my boots aren't handmade, but I've always wanted a pair. You're from Austin?"

"A town near Austin," I say. "And in answer to your first question, I'm Ruby Rothman."

He puts his hand out. "Gus Goren."

No wedding ring, I notice.

"Off the bus, all." Whatever version of Essie Sue they have in the state of Washington has just made her wishes known through a bullhorn as we pulled up at the station. "We're boarding by groups," she says, "and each choir's leader has your tickets."

Gus gets off first, and takes my hand as I jump from the high step.

For once, I'm struggling for words — even though I'm suppressing plenty of silent curses for the short length of the bus trip.

"Brief conversation," I finally say.

"To be continued," he says. "I'll just look for the dark red curls."

26

Amazing what a pick-me-up a brief flirtation can be, especially on a trip that's been a big fat zero so far. On second thought, I'd call last night's shopping excursion with Essie Sue a *minus* zero, and cocktails with Bart Goldman not much better.

The first person I see from our group is André.

"Come on, Ruby, they're about to board," he says. Before I know what's happening, he grabs my hand and rushes me around the corner, where Essie Sue is waving her list. He holds my hand a little too long for comfort. Unfortunately, it's the same hand Gus Goren just held, and I'm foolishly annoyed about that, as if André had ruined it.

"You missed my orientation," she says as I shake off André's grip.

"Why don't you and André start off in seats 15A and B," she says, "since you're the only ones not aboard yet. We can all change around at will, once the conductor has passed through."

Well, that's a blessing — I won't be stuck with him. I try to switch gears, though, and go into business mode, since I did promise to see what's up with André. I make a real effort to put the handholding incident out of my mind, and I give him what I hope passes for a smile of contentment at being his temporary seatmate. André's not a pushover by any means — I've known that for a while now. My real job's going to be to find that fine line between being merely an inquisitive friend and another prospective notch in his belt.

As we walk to the red, white, and blue tour train, we run the gauntlet of uniformed greeters lined up by the tour company to give us a proper send-off. André tries to hurry me along again, but I'm savvy this time, and I avoid any offered appendages.

"Sorry you didn't get to sit with your quartet buddies," I say as we find our seats.

He responds with what I've already noticed is a seduction smile — a flash of white teeth that's supposed to mow us ladies down in Latin-lover style.

"Why, Ruby," he says, "I'm surprised you can even think such a thing. I've wanted to get to know you better for a long, long time.

I can always see the choir people. You and I have to make a serious effort to go deeper on this trip. We need to share."

"Fair enough," I say. "You know, André, I don't know you or your wife very well, and I'd like to learn more about the Korman family. Where did you meet Sara?"

Ha — silly of me to think that any mention of Sara would throw a pro like André. He's not that easily discouraged, or distracted. Although on another level, he just seems to be going through the motions for the sake of habit.

"Sara and I grew up together," he says, "but she's home this trip, and I'm sure you and I have other things to talk about."

"Surely not more important things?" I say.

"How about you?" he says, ignoring my goading. "I've heard you've been a widow for quite a while now. Do you like to go out and have a good time? A trip like this is the time to do that."

"Well, now that we're on this train, I doubt we'll be out and about that much — I think it's mostly group activities on the agenda."

Since I'm just stringing out the conversation, I don't expect my remarks to be illustrated so soon in living color, but on cue, Essie Sue comes down the aisle with an announcement.

"Morning service, people. As soon as the conductor takes your tickets, I want you to come to the observation car. One of the British Columbia groups is leading the worship."

Since our tickets have already been punched, I'm the first to jump up and reach for my handbag.

"Coming?" I say.

André flashes me a half-amused, half-smug smile and joins me. He certainly exudes confidence — in a smarmy sort of way, as if to let me know he'll reel me in later.

We make our way to the observation car, where at least fifty people are trying to squeeze into as little space as possible.

"Hey, Ruby, want to sit here?" Kevin and Bitsy are sharing a space for two with one other person already, but Bitsy jumps happily into Kevin's lap and gestures for me to take her seat. I'm sure I've lost André in the melee, but no such luck — I see him picking his way through the car. Since I have no intention of sharing laps with him, of all people, I'm hoping he finds another place to sit. As I thank Bitsy for the seat she's offered me, I look around to see if Gus might be in this car, but no such luck.

I'm glad we're having the service so soon, since from what I've heard, the scenery gets more gorgeous with every mile east through the Canadian Rockies. ChoirFest or not, I don't intend to miss the spectacular scenery because some Essie Sue type is blocking the view as she lectures the group.

A choir from Victoria is in charge of what they're calling a creative service. I hate to say it, but they're not much better than our choir, although with everyone joining in, the total effect isn't bad. I had hoped, though, that we could learn a lot from these groups — maybe the choirs from the larger congregations will provide some inspiration.

I feel a finger touching the back of my neck. This could only be André — anyone else would tap my shoulder.

"Hey," I say, "don't do that."

"Just wanted you to know where I was," he says, "right here behind you."

He's positioned himself next to my ear, and throughout the service, I'm treated to a critique of the proceedings.

"This is their idea of a meditation?" he says after a period of silent prayer. "They have no idea how to reach the meditative state."

I listen to him for a minute or two, trying to get a clue as to where he's coming from, but I can't take it for too long.

"André, I can't concentrate with you talking in my ear," I turn around to tell him. "Can you wait until after the service? I'd like to talk with you about it then." Irene Cohn is beside him.

"André's right, Ruby," she says, "this isn't creative, it's tedious, just like —"

I poke her with my elbow before she can criticize Kevin right to his face. He gives me a grateful look.

"Our choir's better than this," Bitsy says, nestling into Kevin's lap. "Rabbi Kapstein's a genius."

I wouldn't go that far, or even half that far, but Kevin's glowing.

I excuse myself as soon as the service is over, and take off for the next coach car before anyone can realize I'm gone. If André does try to follow me, I'll duck into the nearest bathroom — although I don't want to discourage him completely before I can find out more about the meditations.

I'm encouraged by the fact that quite a few people are using their cell phones. I felt sure that mine wouldn't work out here, but I'll give it a try. With the crazy hours this morning, I haven't been in touch with Paul, and I told him I'd call.

I ring his cell and reach him at the station.

"Hi, hon," he says. "What's up?"

"Just wanted to keep in touch," I say, "nothing really to report. We're on the train already, and I've tried to make some conversation with André Korman. He's criticizing the services, but nothing other than that. I'm hoping he might lead me to something more that might have been spooking Serena."

"Don't be heavy-handed, Ruby, not in that closed-in atmosphere."

"Give me credit for more than that, Paul — it's hard enough just to spend five minutes with him. I'm wasting most of my time trying to avoid the guy, so I'm doing this in small segments."

I don't think it's necessary to mention his coming on to me, but Paul does.

"Remember what a womanizer he is."

"Yeah, I know."

I hope Paul doesn't start with the jealousy bit — we've made no commitments, and yet he's barely gotten over my dating Ed. How he could even think I'd respond to André's pathetic moves, I'll never know.

"What's going on at home?" I ask. It's difficult to hear him, and as usual during the day, he's talking to me at the same time he's being distracted by someone there at the station.

"Aside from finding out Serena was poisoned, not much is happening," he says. "Of course, that's a big deal in itself."

"But who do you think knows that here?" I say. "Anyone?"

"I don't want you finding out," he says. "Bart Goldman's still close to Joellyn, and it's possible she might have told him. But it could be dangerous for you to ask about this."

"I spoke to Bart last night," I say, neglecting to say I had drinks with him. Or that he seemed interested in me. Why get Paul upset about nothing?

"Did he say anything?"

"Nothing about that. I pumped him a bit about Joellyn, and he didn't say he'd been in touch yesterday, which is the only day he could have learned about the poisoning. But he does think Rose should have never gone to Ohio."

"I'm in touch with Joellyn off and on about the case," Paul says. "Maybe I can ask if she's emailed or phoned Bart — or anyone else, for that matter."

"Yeah," I say, "it *would* be nice to find out who knows what —"

"Before you go barging in and put yourself

in a dangerous situation," Paul says.

"That wasn't what I was going to say, Paul. You didn't even let me finish my sentence — what's that all about?"

"I'd feel safer if I were up there directing things," he says.

I fight my inclination to chafe at that. It's irritating, but then Paul *is* the professional and I'm not. I still hate it, though, that he's glad to have the extra eyes and ears I can provide, yet he won't give me credit for good judgment. And to make things worse, he's having this conversation while other people there are probably standing around listening.

"Let's hang up before we get into a fight," I say. "I'm doing the best I can."

I guess we're of like mind, because someone says something to him and he's off the phone before I can say a proper good-bye, whatever that would be.

27

At least I'm not missing the scenery — we're passing through the area of the great salmon runs, and I see two gigantic swing span bridges out the window. The steward told me the natives of this region paddled below us centuries ago on their way up-stream for the salmon harvest. We can even see Mount Baker in Washington State from here, and I hear we're scheduled to pass through several tunnels along Fraser Canyon.

"Can I sit by you for a few minutes, Ruby? I didn't read the guidebook, and you're always up on these things."

It's Kevin.

"Sure, but where's Bitsy?" I ask.

"Essie Sue needed her for something."

"How's it going?"

"Okay. Bitsy can be a little tiring — she's always so chipper."

"But that's who she is, Kevin. If chipper's

not good, you might as well know it now."

"There's one good thing," he says. "When she's around, there's no room for me to think about a lot of other stuff that bothers me."

"That's good?"

"Well, yeah — she's distracting. It's just that I get exhausted from it."

"So mix a little. Try to meet people besides the Eternal contingent. That's what travel's all about."

"I haven't done that yet, but I did hang around Irene Cohn for a while. She's kind of weird, don't you think?"

"In what way?"

"At home, she's always rolling her eyes during services when I preach. I can see her to my left in the choir section."

"Then why would you want to talk to her on vacation?"

"I heard her complaining to André and Bart about how dull the service was, and how it was like ours at home. She said something to André about Serena that I didn't understand, and he seemed to be angry with her. So she went over and sat with me, though I can't imagine why. I thought maybe I could talk to her and she'd like me more."

"Well, it never hurts to go out of your way

with congregants if you have a ready-made opportunity. What did she say?"

"Not much. She was still fuming over whatever the argument was with André, and maybe she wanted him to notice that she had someone else to talk to. I was just in a convenient spot. I asked her to tell me why she didn't like the service this morning."

"What did she say?"

"That's the weird part. She asked if I even had a clue about the preparation for real prayer, but then she seemed sorry she said it and backed off."

"What do you mean, backed off?"

"She looked over the aisle at Bart and André and said I shouldn't pay any attention to what she was saying — that she was in a bad mood. But I decided I wouldn't let it go at that. I asked her to get together with me sometime so we could make services better."

"Good for you. Did she respond?"

"She looked at me and said it was probably too late for that. Then she backed off *that* and said maybe we would all meet — that she'd talk to André about it."

"Did you happen to ask her what she said to André about Serena?"

"No, but I did mention Serena. I said their little group must miss Serena, because I'd noticed that the quartet was always very close, and that Serena must have been a big part of that. I told her I was sorry I couldn't have talked with Serena about services, too."

"That's interesting."

"What's so interesting? I was only doing what you just now said I should do, Ruby — trying to go out of my way for her. Serena's dead — my chance to know her better is gone."

I'm in a quandary here — I can't confide too much in Kevin, but if I could encourage him to open up even more to this group, he could be really helpful to me. I'm just not sure how to do that.

"I think you should continue the conversation whenever you can, Kevin. And I can't imagine why the subject of Serena should be off-limits, do you? I wonder what André was so uptight about."

"Ruby, why does everyone always talk around me, as if they're keeping things from me? You're doing it, too. What's up with Serena?"

"I can't say, Kevin. Do you think you could trust me to ask you to keep your ears open when you're talking to what's left of the quartet? I promise you I'll fill you in when I can."

"You're interested in Serena because . . . ?"

"I can't say anything else. Will you go along with me?" I know I'm taking a risk here that he'll tell someone I asked him to eavesdrop, but I decide to do it anyway.

"I guess I'll go along, whatever that means," he says. "You know I'm always the last to find out stuff, so I don't know what help I'm going to be to you."

"I don't either, but let's leave it at that just the same."

They're bringing around a yummy lunch on the train — a big piece of cold poached salmon, lots of salad greens, and some marinated vegetables. I'm remembering the days when we suffered through the all-white airline lunches of taco pie, rice, white rolls, and vanilla pudding — what an improvement. The car steward pours some Chardonnay from a Pacific Northwest winery I'm not familiar with, and it's excellent, not to mention the strawberries topped with powdered sugar.

Lunch is perfect for ten minutes, until Essie Sue finds me.

"Ruby, you know that most of our group is staying at a hotel in Kamloops tonight, don't you?"

"I hadn't thought about it," I say. "Why?"

"Well, you and I have been offered a complimentary roomette on the train, and I think we should take it as a leadership perk. We deserve it."

"If the train's starting out from Kamloops tomorrow, how can we stay aboard tonight when everyone else is at a hotel?" I say. "We'll be way ahead of them."

"The train won't be moving tonight — it will wait for the group. The bedroom's just a bonus."

"Huh? You mean we get to swap a roomy hotel room for a stationary little cabin just because it's on the train? That's a perk?"

"Come see it with me — you'll love it."

I bring along a brownie from my lunch tray and she drags me to one of the roomettes in the bedroom car. As I expected, it's smaller than the cabin on a bargain cruise, and I'm an expert on those.

"You can stand on my bed to get to yours," she says.

"Meaning you get the lower bunk," I say.

"I'm the one they're complimenting by this offer, Ruby, so of course I get the bottom bed."

"So far," I say, "you haven't even been able to close the door behind you. How will you fit your luggage in, much less me?"

Before she's even finished squeezing the

door shut, claustrophobia sets in. The thought of Essie Sue's normal intrusive presence bouncing off these walls is enough to set my teeth on edge.

"No, I'm declining," I say. "Thanks, anyway."

"But it will save us the cost of a hotel room," she says. "This is free."

"I'll pay for my hotel room if you stay here," I assure her. "Free's not always what it's cracked up to be."

It's not easy to get out of a room that barely holds both of us, but when my sanity's at stake, I'm pretty efficient.

"I'm outta here," I say. "We'll connect tomorrow."

"No, if you're not staying, I'm not, either — we can keep one another company tonight to keep our spirits up. I'm sure this little pit stop isn't what we're used to in Eternal."

"Kamloops? It's not a pit stop, and it has gorgeous views. There are some great restaurants here, too. Eternal should have so much to offer."

"All right, we'll stay with the rest of the group," she says. I guess I'm not off the hook after all. But just because we're rooming together doesn't mean I have to spend my days with her.

"See you later," I say, heading the other way, through the observation car. The cocktail lounge is in here, too, and the waiters are setting up for business this afternoon, I guess. I'm about to cut through to find our group, when I see André, Irene, and Bart. They're huddled together in a far corner, and they're so intent on whatever they're doing that they don't even see me coming through.

I take the nearest seat so that we're still separated by the length of the car. Irene and André are leading some sort of chant, while swaying with their eyes closed. It'd probably be a good idea to be doing something if they notice me, so I carefully take a paperback out of my leather carryall. Not carefully enough, apparently, because a map I'd put between the book's pages falls into the aisle at the same time, and I instinctively reach down to grab it.

They see me.

28

"Who's that?" André says, looking around.

"It's Ruby over there." Irene, already standing, points my way.

"Hi," I say. "I thought I'd read by these sunny windows for a while. Am I disturbing you? If so, I can move."

When I'm unexpectedly discovered somewhere, I always announce my presence with a question — it's a good distraction.

"No, don't be silly," Irene says. "We're just having a meeting. You can read while we . . ."

It becomes obvious to everyone, though, that they can't, or won't, continue while I'm reading.

"Why don't you join us?" André says. "You might find this interesting."

"I can see I'm intruding — why don't I come back some other time?" I say.

"It's nothing secret," Irene says, to André's obvious annoyance.

"Why would you say that?" he asks her. "Of course it's nothing secret — come on over, Ruby."

"Yeah, come on," Bart says.

I step over to the semicircular booth they're occupying. Irene sits down and lets André take over.

"We're meditating," he says. "A sort of group meditation. We find that these prayers are a way to lead us down to a place of greater spiritual depth."

"Greater than what?" I say.

"Than ordinary modern methods of worship. It's not easy to explain to . . ."

"To someone who's barged in," I say. "I understand — that's why I didn't want to break in on a private meeting."

"André can explain it to you," Irene says. "It's much more than a worship experience. It's his way of giving us directions to the right path."

Bart seems embarrassed for some reason — he can't quite look at me.

"You mean André's directing?" I ask, glancing over at Bart anyway. "Do you all take turns?"

"Not me," Bart finally says. "I don't know much about this."

"Are you using a prayer book?" I say.

"It's not needed," André says. "If you'll

stop asking questions and let yourself be a part of the flow, it will come to you."

André pulls me down into the seat beside him — now I'm squeezed between him and Bart, with Irene facing me at the other side of the curved table.

"Can we spread out a bit?" I say. "There's nowhere to put my hands." Or arms, either. And André's sitting too close to me for comfort. I notice that all three of them have their hands on the table — I'm tempted to ask where the Ouija board is, but I hold it in. This is no place for humor — especially not my brand.

Everyone moves over, but apparently not far enough for Irene, who's also noticed André's proximity and is glaring at me.

"I can't stay long," I say. "I really don't want to miss this gorgeous scenery."

"Ruby," André says, "you have no idea what you're missing besides the scenery. Don't you ever think about the unseen?"

"Usually not in a group," I say. "I'm flawed."

"But the group energy is very important. We pray silently — like the Quakers, but our content is biblical."

Biblical? I'm dubious, but I'm not about to interrupt at this point. I want to see what's going on here.

"We can't fully demonstrate it here on the train," Irene says, "but you need to understand that everything we do is connected."

"Like to the universe?" I say.

"No, to Los Angeles."

"That's the corporate headquarters of Jewish Mystic Central," André tells me. "We get praying aids from them, cards printed with the chants, CDs, DVDs, bracelets — you name it, they have it."

"Retail and wholesale," Irene says.

"Wholesale?" I say. "And you've kept this a secret from Essie Sue? She lives for that."

"Essie Sue wouldn't understand," Irene says. "This is a cutting-edge movement, Ruby. Essie Sue's too mainstream, and besides, she'd want to take it over the way she does everything else around temple."

"We're basically a leaderless operation, Ruby," André says. "That's the way it should be — each finding his or her own right way."

"But I thought Irene said you were the one pointing to the right path," I say.

"I am, but only until everyone catches up with me. I'm on a different spiritual level right now."

"Let me get back to the wholesale-retail level," I say. "Tell me again how you heard about this?"

"Through my business," he says. "You know we carry a lot of wellness material in the health food store. There was an ad about the new spirituality, and about this movement that's attracting as many of those out of the faith as in the faith. It's for everyone — even the movie stars are into it. They buy a lot of the bracelets."

"You mean like Lance Armstrong's yellow bracelets?" I say.

"Yes, but these aren't for charity. They *are* charity."

"I'm getting it," I say. "It's kind of like a franchise?"

"Well, if I launch this correctly, I could be the Central Texas distributor. But that's not the main point — the higher message is to reach the depths of prayer. The stuff they sell only represents the physical manifestation of this — like a study aid."

"And if you introduced this to Temple Rita as an organization, they would be able to use the profits to help the congregation do its work, right?" I say. "Like Essie Sue usually does?"

"That's the last thing I want to do," he says. "She wouldn't understand. And neither would the rabbi. This is more individual than congregational."

You can say that again.

"So you'd get the profits?" I say.

"To further my work," he says.

I look over at Bart. *Et tu?* I say.

"Honestly, Ruby, this is the first time I've ever heard him talk about profits. It wasn't his emphasis. You really do need to learn more about this — it's complex."

"Very complex, Ruby," Irene says. "You have no idea how uplifting these meditations are. If Essie Sue and the temple board could look beyond what Rabbi Kapstein is doing, they could see that this represents the future."

"Maybe, but whose?" I say. This sounds all about André's future.

"I knew you shouldn't have invited Ruby over to our table, André," Irene says. "She's not the type to understand deeper spirituality. And now she could ruin everything. Just like . . ."

"Whoa," I say. "What *everything*? And like who? What kind of plans do you have? We're talking Eternal, Texas, folks, not the dawn of a new world."

André takes a deep breath and puts his hand on top of mine on the seat between us. I instinctively pull it off like a hot coal, but he's undeterred.

"Ruby, we've always been good friends."

Not.

"This is a very sacred moment," he says. "We think enough of you to want you to be a part of something transformational and, as Dr. Goldman says, complex. Will you promise us not to speak to anyone else about these matters until we've oriented you properly?"

I agree with him that they're a disorienting bunch, but if I'm not careful, I'll make an enemy of these people way before I need to. I think of Paul and back off.

"Sure. Orient me. I'm game."

André and Irene visibly relax. I don't think Bart Goldman is as persuaded, but he's so conflicted about my seeing him in this situation that his embarrassment is calling the shots. He shrugs and looks away.

"Will you come to one of our hotel rooms and hear more?" André says. "Irene and Bart will be there, too," he reassures me. "How about tonight? Or tomorrow morning? We're meeting both times."

"Let's play it by ear tonight," I say. "I'm not even sure where I'm staying yet."

"But you won't say anything?" Irene asks.

"That's taken for granted, Irene," André says. "Ruby said she'll wait."

"No," Irene says, "she said she'll let you orient her."

Orient me? This is beginning to sound

pornographic.

"Yeah, yeah," I say to all. "I'll keep your secret."

André flares up again. "It's not —"

"I know," I say. "It's a secret but it's not. Whatever it is, I won't say anything until I understand more.

"How about letting me out?" I push toward Bart as the lesser of the evils. "I'll leave so you can all talk about me."

"Of course we won't discuss you," André says as I get up. "We wouldn't think of it."

"It's a joke," I say.

But I have a feeling it won't be for long.

29

We connected with the Canadian Pacific Railway tracks a while back, and our train roars in and out of the tunnels along Fraser Canyon. I love the sudden blackness followed by the bright flash that means daylight is back again. What a waste to spend time in futile conversation with Mystic Central when I could have been taking pictures like mad with my little Minolta digital, no bigger than a deck of cards. Some of our Eternal group are leaning out between the car couplings to take photos in the fresh air instead of through the glassed-in train windows. I've been thinking of walking up to the engine area to take some shots from the front end of the train, if they'll let me.

There's no way to reach the scenic area we're traveling through except by train or trekking through with a backpack. The highways cut straight through less interesting country for efficiency's sake, while the railroad was planned to take advantage of the spectacular backcountry views. Nan would love this.

Now that I'm cars away from anyone I know, I grab an empty window seat and call Paul. We're not that far from Kamloops, so I'm hoping I'm not too isolated to get through to his cell.

"Hi, hon. It's me."

"Ruby? I can hardly hear you."

"Where are you?"

"I'm in the Starbucks drive-through line," he says, "on my way to check out a crime scene. This is a perfect time to get me."

"I'd be jealous of your latte if I hadn't just feasted on some good Pacific Northwest coffee with country cream."

"What's country about your cream? Aren't all cows rural?"

"I won't answer that, smarty-pants. Miss me?"

"You bet. What's up? I hope you're watching your back."

"Well, since you're not here to watch it, I have to, right? I was wondering if you'd called Joellyn in Ohio. You said you might."

"Yeah, I did. I asked her if she'd contacted anyone since she found out her sister was poisoned. She said she'd emailed Dr. Goldman, as part of a regular email correspondence they have. He must have received the message yesterday, since she said she'd just sent it and hadn't had an answer. I don't think she expects one — she seems to think he won't be able to be in touch that often up there. She just wanted to keep him posted."

"That's interesting. I spent some time chatting with him and he didn't say anything, even though we pretty much covered the waterfront when we talked. He even mentioned Joellyn by name, but didn't tell me that."

I'm still not informing Paul we chatted it up in a cocktail lounge.

"He could have logged on after talking with you, Ruby — maybe at the hotel at night."

"You're right. But I saw him today, too — we're all together here in fairly close quarters."

"Not so odd, I guess," Paul says. "Maybe he just told people he's closer with than you."

"That's a distinct possibility."

We had quite an intimate conversation over cognac last night, but Bart was like an entirely different person today in the observation car. I still can't get over *that* encounter.

"I'm here at the crime scene," Paul says. "Gotta go."

"Can I call you back?"

"I'll try to get you later. I'm still worried, though — have you cut it too close with anyone you're not telling me about? I know how you are when you're hound-dogging something."

"I'm being careful. But after what you've told me about Bart, I'm wondering who's making an end run around whom."

"Later, babe, okay?"

He hangs up before I can answer or say that I miss him. I put my phone in my jacket pocket and stare out the window for a while as we fly by beautiful waterfalls and white-water rafting spots. I'd love to be photographing this, but instead I'm sitting here wondering if Bart told his friends André and Irene the latest about Serena. And I thought I was so cleverly scoping him out last night. Apparently, he's way ahead of me.

"Hi, Ruby, we're just car-hopping. Can we sit with you?"

Kevin and Bitsy take the two seats facing me.

"I don't like riding backwards," Bitsy says. She moves over beside me and then asks,

"Can you let the rabbi sit by me, too?"

"Huh?" I say.

"You know — like swap with him. So we can be together."

This is vintage Bitsy — the word *passive-aggressive* was invented for people like this. And the reason she's so successful at it is that no one wants to take the trouble to pick it apart. Except me.

"Why didn't you just ask me at the beginning to give up my good seat to the two of you," I say, "instead of trying to extract it by degrees?"

"Would you have?" she says.

"No."

"I don't blame you," she says. "That would have been pushy of us."

"Us? I didn't see Kevin asking."

"It's just that once I got over here in your seat, I started missing him, and I thought you'd understand, being another girl and all."

"I was wondering how long it would take you to blame this on me," I say. "Exactly thirty seconds."

"That's not fair," she says.

"What's not fair?" I ask her. "You've got a fair choice — you can ride backwards and hold hands with Kevin, or sit by me, not get dizzy, and look at Kevin across from you."

She stays put. The only thing wrong with this picture is that she's already won, because at the most I'll only be able to tolerate her for a few minutes before having to move. Which was the point, I guess.

"Hey, Ruby," Kevin says, "remember you asked me to keep my eyes and ears open whenever I was around the quartet?"

The cliché would be that my heart sinks at that, but actually what's sinking is any hope that I'll ever be able to treat this man like a friend who might do a favor for me without blowing it.

I try to ignore this by gathering my backpack off the floor in preparation for leaving the scene, but he doesn't let me.

"Remember?" he says.

I look at Bitsy, there on alert, but he still doesn't get it that this was between the two of us. On the other hand, I don't want Bitsy making too much of this — she could then blab to Essie Sue and company. None of my choices is good, so I plunge in.

"Yeah, I remember. It's not important."

I start to get up.

"Well, I saw them just now before Bitsy ran into me, and we visited for a few minutes."

Bitsy's not missing a word.

"That's nice," I say, standing.

"No, don't go," he says. "I have to tell you what happened."

Now I'm really caught — I want to know, but not in front of Bitsy. And I can't say so without indicating that this might be important to me. Not to mention that if I leave, he's going to tell her anyway.

I sit down.

"Remember that last time I saw Irene, she said she'd speak to André about services at Temple Rita, and that she'd ask him if the quartet would discuss it with me sometime? Well, when I ran into them just now, I asked her in front of André if she'd spoken to him."

"Just temple politics," I say to Bitsy. "I was encouraging Kevin to get to know the congregants more informally on this trip."

"So anyway, Ruby," Kevin continues, "Irene seemed embarrassed. I thought you'd be interested in that. And André accused her of blabbing to too many people. Namely me, I guess."

I nod, waiting for him to go on. There's nothing I can say to get out of this hole, anyway.

"André said I was the last person Irene needed to talk to. I tried to help out Irene by saying that you'd encouraged me to open up more to the quartet — that it wasn't just Irene's fault."

Oy. This is worse than I thought. Now the quartet won't confide in me at all. André's no fool, and he'll know I wanted Kevin to soak up any information he could. The irony is that I couldn't care less about their secret spiritual quest if I didn't think one of them might be a murderer.

30

Email to: Nan
From: Ruby
Subject: Hi from Kamloops

Hey — found an Internet café here at the train station near Kamloops — odd name, huh? It's an Indian name for "meeting of the waters" — this is the convergence of the North and South Thompson rivers. You'd love it here, babe — we just passed a huge osprey nest on top of a telephone pole near an abandoned mill. I saw one of them swooping straight down to the water, on the lookout for fish. This might even beat what we saw on our trip to Alaska — I think this is a better season for spotting wildlife.

An update to what I told you on the phone — we're pretty sure that Serena's ex, Dr. Bart Goldman, knows that the autopsy showed she'd been poisoned, but he's said nothing to me about it, even though we've talked.

By the way, did I tell you I met a cute guy on our way out of Vancouver the other day? He's one of the Washington contingent, and I hope I'll run into him at the conference.

Email to: Ruby
From: Nan
Subject: How's that again?

What cute guy? I thought your cute guy quotient was filled. Tell all, even if there isn't much. And by the way, are you and Paul getting along on the phone? Remember what I told you about long-distance misunderstandings — things can get twisted on the phone in a way they wouldn't in person. I'm not all that happy to hear that your eye is roving, Ruby.

RE the autopsy information, you might be operating at a disadvantage. One of these characters could be a killer, and if I were you, I'd be glad no one's talked about this. If the wrong person found out you're in possession of damaging information, you could be caught upstream at those rivers of yours without a you-know-what. I'm not there to get your back, and Paul's not, either.

Speaking of loose tongues, Essie Sue hasn't heard the latest about Serena, has she?

Email to: Nan
From: Ruby
Subject: It's all cool

The cute guy is Gus Goren, and we just flirted a bit — and by that I mean for about sixty seconds — honest. But as for my roving eye quotient, or whatever you said, why shouldn't I? I'm not dead yet, and I'm still single, despite your attempts to couple me so soon after the Ed fiasco. I know you like Paul a lot, and he's still the main man, I guess, but this is exactly why I'm not committed, Nan.

Essie Sue doesn't know that Serena was poisoned, but I'm more worried about Kevin. I asked him to keep his ears open when he was around those people in Serena's quartet, and I think he blurted something out to them about my request. This is only going to make it harder for me to get tight with them. They're into some sort of user—friendly version of Kabbalistic practice, and I'm trying to find out what's going on there. I'll keep you updated.

Email to: Ruby
From: Nan
Subject: Uneasy

You're not exactly decreasing my anxiety level. What's keeping you from waiting to explore the circumstances surrounding Serena's death when you get back home to Eternal? You'll have police support and you won't be exposing yourself in unfamiliar territory.

By the way, Ruby, stop confiding in Kevin.

Okay, I accept your single status and your right to connect with a neat guy, but I guess I am prejudiced in Paul's favor. Only be careful — and not just with the romance. Wish I were there with you, because my Ruby antennae (and you *know* they're accurate) are buzzing all over the place.

Email to: Nan
From: Ruby
Subject: I'm perfectly safe

I promise I'll take care of myself. And if I need to make a quick retreat, you're just over the border in Seattle, right?

31

It's a shame to have to look forward to a night as Essie Sue's roommate after dining at a great restaurant with a spectacular view of Kamloops below us. The two bottles of wine our table shared are taking their toll, though, and I don't really have to be persuaded to head home to bed — if sleep is possible with Essie Sue in the room. I want to get up early tomorrow morning to catch the meditation service — it's in Irene's hotel room. The three-legged quartet has reminded me to drop in before we take the train for the second lap of our journey.

"No midnight pajama party," I say to Essie Sue in the taxi. "I need my sleep. You'll have to watch the shopping channels on your own."

"Oh, they probably don't even have them here," she says, unwilling to admit that this isn't the boonies. "Besides, I have a surprise for us that doesn't involve television."

I'm too drowsy to take the bait, but I rouse myself when we get back to our room and I discover that my flannel PJs are missing. Essie Sue puts on a three-piece silk lounging ensemble in pale peach.

"Too bad Hal's not here to enjoy this," she says. "I picked it up in Vancouver — they have some very sophisticated boutiques."

I'm amused, though I'm not sure why. "Hal, huh?" I say. "So he's still interested? Good for him."

"Well, I wouldn't say *interested* exactly," she says, "but he says he's always glad when I go to bed happy."

That, I can believe. But since she brought up this topic, I can't quite let it go.

"So do you two still — uh — get it on in the romance department?"

"Hal's past his prime," she says. "I got him samples of Viagra, but he refused to take it, even when we watched the ads together. He said it had side effects. I pointed out to him how self-confident those men on TV looked, with their wives adoringly gazing up at them. Like Nancy Reagan."

"It didn't fly?"

"He said it wouldn't work with him — he was a registered Democrat. I'm not giving up, though. I'm bringing back one of those DVDs of *Massage for Lovers* — even though he's never been very good with his hands. He can't even drive a nail in the wall."

I don't go there.

"Okay, Essie Sue," I say, "where did you hide my pajamas?"

"Not *hide,* dear, *eliminate.* You deserve better, and that's part of my surprise for tonight."

She brings out a plastic shopping bag and pours onto my bed what appears to be an exact replica of her outfit, except for the color. Mine's in slinky black, but it still looks like something Vanity Fair made in 1955.

"Yours isn't silk," she says, "it's rayon, but I knew you'd insist on throwing it into the washing machine, so I didn't waste the money."

"I thought you said I deserved better," I say. "I'll freeze in this. Just tell me where you eliminated my PJs."

"They're gone," she says. "And this surprise isn't just for you, Ruby. It's a step toward your future. Others are involved."

I don't want to know this.

"I'm exhausted, Essie Sue. And this hotel room doesn't even have terry-cloth robes."

At this point, I head for the bathroom. I

refuse to waste another hour on this. The outfit turns out to be not only slippery but cold — like I'm wearing someone else's skin. Someone who's not a mammal.

"Beautiful," she says when I come out. "Get used to it — and look what I've collected for you."

She's sitting on my bed with a computer on her lap, plugged in and ready to go.

"I downloaded these five for you from the Internet," she says, "and they're all Jewish. I saved it all on a DVD to show you here."

The Nu — a Jew for You logo comes up, followed by photos and bios. When I take the laptop, the electricity from my faux-sateen outfit almost shorts out the computer, but I'm not so lucky.

"This is Maury Blumenfeld," she says, showing me number one. Maury's seen better days, looking about as confident as I feel in black rayon, and appearing a little Viagra-deprived himself, if I'm any judge.

"His bio's very interesting," Essie Sue says. "He's a doctor."

"No," I point out, "he has a doctorate in lawn improvement from University World Online. There's a difference."

Sleepy as I am, I find myself weirdly fascinated by the pickings she's laid out. And besides, she's on my bed.

"Maury Blumenfeld's probably not his real name," Essie Sue tells me.

"Yeah, I'm aware of that," I say. If that's the best pseudonym he could come up with, I wonder what the real thing is. Not that I should expect much ingenuity from a doctor of lawn improvement.

"Next is Jerrold Oshman," she says. "He likes his women smart but not too smart, wild, and undemanding. You'd have to work on being undemanding, Ruby."

"Thanks for the two-thirds compliment," I say. "I think. Sounds like every man's fantasy to me. Lots of luck to Jerrold."

I don't bother to bring up Jerrold's graphic, but then, I'm pretty undemanding when the occasion calls for it. Instead, I flip to number three, Isaac Epps.

"How old are these guys, Essie Sue?" I ask after taking a look.

"I told them you would accept any age," she says.

That explains it. Isaac's photo should be in sepia — he looks like he's fleeing the Russian army. Under the czars.

"Only two more, right?" I say.

"Don't go so fast," she says, "these were the cream of the crop in your category."

"You mean the 'I'll take anything' category?" I say. "I shudder to imagine how you described me."

The competitive part of me is already thinking how a little creativity could bring up a much better rogues' gallery, but right now my goal is to go to bed. Alone.

Theo Tamarkin, number four, is posing with a whip.

"I think this whip still has the price tag on it, Essie Sue," I say. "Is this what they mean by Jewish S-and-M?"

"I thought he seemed a bit more stimulating than some of the others," she says.

Uh-oh. I don't want to go there, either. Poor Hal.

"Now I remember why I picked him," she says. "Theo had an unusual philosophy of life. He said he wanted a generous wife with a good job, and he would only get married in a warm community-property state. Since Texas is a warm community-property state, I thought this would work to your advantage."

"Or most certainly to his," I say. "I think we can safely delete Theo."

I'm about to rush through number five, when I do a double take. On the screen, with captions from the site, in living color, is my ex-boyfriend Ed Levinger. And to add insult to whatever else is injuring me regarding Ed, his quite adorable color photo was taken by *moi.*

"You're kidding," I say, now totally awake. "Where did you get this?"

"Well, I admit it wasn't in your former-rabbi's-wife category," she says, "but I was browsing and ran into it. I wanted to prove to you that you never know who's doing on-line dating."

"So where's his bio?" I say.

"I only downloaded the photo, since you already know his biographical profile. Shall we go to sleep now?"

32

My attempt to leave without waking Essie
Sue doesn't work, so I tell her I have to go
to Irene Cohn's room to get a book I'm bor-
rowing.

"I didn't know you two were friends," she
says. "She doesn't seem like your type."

"We're not what I'd call *friends*," I say,
"she's someone I know from temple. What's
the big deal? And while we're at it, what *is*
my type?"

"Oh, you know — eccentric. You pick odd
people."

Talk about the pot calling the kettle *eccentric.*

"We can talk about my oddball friends
some other time," I say, "gotta go. I'll see
you on the train."

"But aren't you coming to the box breakfast on the bus that takes us to the train?
We worked so hard on it while the rest of
you were out to dinner last night."

"I didn't see any box breakfast on the schedule. What's that?"

"It was an unscheduled opportunity, and I grabbed it. I found out that the hotel had ham roll-ups left over from a big buffet last night that apparently didn't draw as many people as expected. The manager told me we could get them at a bargain price if we wanted them, but of course there was the ham problem. So a few people I organized spent a couple of hours taking the ham out of the roll-ups and replacing it with cottage cheese. We left the celery and the parsley in. I thought cottage cheese roll-ups would be perfect for breakfast as a surprise treat. You won't miss it, will you?"

" 'Fraid so," I say. This is one unscheduled opportunity I'm definitely passing up. I just hope no one gets ptomaine from it — that's all we need.

The door to Irene's room has been left ajar, and I slip in just as she, André, and Bart are beginning the service, or whatever they're calling it. The curtains are drawn in the living room and no lights are on, so I'm hoping not to attract any unnecessary attention. The three of them are there, plus two other people I've never seen — other invitees from the train trip, I guess.

I hear familiar Hebrew melodies being

played on a portable CD player, and they're all sitting cross-legged in a circle on the floor. Despite my tiptoeing, André notices me and waves me over — the rest of them have their eyes closed.

"We're giving ourselves a buzz before the hectic pace of the day," he whispers.

Nothing wrong with that, although not being a morning person, the last thing I need at this early hour is a buzz, unless it's from coffee, and I don't smell any being made. I guess this group will be ripe for Essie Sue's roll-ups — something tells me there'll be plenty left.

"This is the creative part of the service," André says. "We aim to go down as deep into our consciousness as we can, and when we come up, we'll express it."

Something tells me this isn't what the rabbis had in mind, but it might have been why they didn't encourage novices to delve into this, either.

After a few minutes of silence, Irene, who has yet to nod to me, passes around a set of plastic-coated cards.

"These are for worshippers who might have a hard time expressing themselves," André says.

"Like a study aid?" I say.

"You'll see," he says. "They're part of the

meditation pack I'm hoping to introduce to selected people, as soon as I get the licensing franchise."

"And this is why this has to be hush-hush?" I say.

"Of course, Ruby. I don't want others taking over before I've even signed the contract. This is like a beta group — we're the cutting-edgers who are testing the waters."

Got it. I'm so much more comfortable when I understand the mechanics. My card contains homilies about the contemplative life — nothing very cutting-edge that I can see.

André's just asked Bart Goldman to read his card when there's a loud knock at the open door — a redundancy that could only escape someone like Kevin.

"Ruby, are you in here?" he says. "It's so dark I can't see anything. Essie Sue said you were headed for Irene's room, and someone steered me toward this corridor."

Irene jumps up, pulls the curtains, and finally acknowledges my presence.

"Ruby, you mean you didn't even have the courtesy to shut the door behind you?" she says.

"I thought you were leaving it open for other people you'd asked," I say. "How was I supposed to know to close it? There was a book there keeping it open."

"For you," André says.

By this time, I'm up on my feet.

"I'll talk to the rabbi outside," I say.

"No, that won't be necessary," André says, standing and gathering the worship aids from the participants. *Gathering* is hardly the right word, though, to describe his actions — he's practically inhaling those cards. Within a couple of seconds, he's pocketed the pack and jerked the CD out of its player. He obviously doesn't know our rabbi that well — Kevin's not exactly fast on the uptake.

Kevin, not surprisingly, is oblivious to everything but what he's come for. He nudges me into a corner away from the others, half of whom are still sitting on the floor wondering why they're not meditating.

"Ruby, I'm representing Temple Rita tonight when we give our introductions at the ChoirFest. Essie Sue said you'd help me with this speech — she wants it to be extra good. Isn't there a bedroom we can use for a few minutes?"

"Why couldn't you wait until we were on the train?" I say. "I don't think your barging in is exactly welcome."

"Because you're always wanting to watch the scenery or take pictures or something," he says. "I wanted you to help me before everything started. I really, really need this, Ruby."

He's awfully excited, even for Kevin. There's an edge to his voice I don't hear very often, and it doesn't make sense that he'd get this panicked over a speech.

"Why are you so nervous?" I ask him. "Meet me in the lobby in a half hour, and I'll help you."

I try to steer him out the door before André has a fit thinking Kevin will discover something. Between the two of them, I'm wishing I were already on the train.

"No," he says.

"Are you telling me this can't wait?" I say.

"No, it can't."

By this point, André's had time to put Irene in charge of silent meditations, sans CD music and accompanying sales products, and he comes over to us. He's obviously had a chance to compose himself now that he's hidden the goods from Kevin, and he even manages one of those creepy smiles of his.

"Can I help, Rabbi? You seem perturbed. Let's go in the bedroom."

Kevin's now more wild-eyed than ever, but he jumps at the chance to go into another room, even with André along.

"That's what I've been asking Ruby to do," he says.

Well, if André's not worried anymore about his little plot being discovered, why should I be? It could be that he wants to see for himself whether or not Kevin observed anything, but that's not a problem, either. I know Kevin. Maybe we can both help him with the speech and get it over with.

We sit him on Irene's bed and pull up two chairs.

"This is okay for André to hear?" Kevin says.

"Yeah," I say, "we can both help you."

"The rabbi's having a problem with the speech he's giving when the conference convenes," I tell André. "Maybe we can give him some ideas."

"Why not?" André says with a look that might as well be a wink. I think that in his new role as meditation guru, he's flattered to be helping the clergy.

"Okay," Kevin says, "if you're sure it's all right to talk to both of you."

"It's fine," I say.

"Ruby, I messed up," he says. "With Essie Sue."

"She's just concerned you won't make a good impression," I say. "Once we get this

241

speech nailed down, she'll be fine."

"You don't understand, Ruby — it isn't the speech. That was just an excuse in front of all those people. I wanted to talk to you about something else that just happened — something I really messed up. I should have come to you about it, but Essie Sue was there and you weren't, and I got upset. You know how she always gets things out of me."

"What could she get out of you?" Even with my brain being caffeine deprived so far this morning, I can't think of anything he knows that she shouldn't. Fortunately, I haven't told him anything about my conversations with Paul.

"Well, this morning I got a call from Sara Bernstein, wanting to know if I could conduct a memorial service for her neighbor's mother who died. The neighbor isn't a member of the temple, so he didn't want to call directly. Anyway, we were making the arrangements, and Sara happened to mention . . ."

Kevin looks at André, then at me. "You know," he says, "she happened to mention some gossip that's going around Eternal. I don't usually repeat gossip, but I saw Essie Sue in the lobby right after my phone call, and she said I looked like I was keeping something from her."

"She knows you pretty well," I say, "so I'm not surprised. But hey, what was it? Unless it was some sort of rabbinical confidence. Is that what you're concerned about? If so, we don't want to know. And Essie Sue should be ashamed of herself for pulling it out of you. That's low, even for her."

"No, it wasn't a rabbinical confidence."

"Then tell us," André says.

"Well, Ruby told me a couple of times that there was nothing wrong with bringing up Serena's name in conversation, so I told Essie Sue what I'd heard from Sara Bernstein, and she flipped."

A shot of pure caffeine couldn't do to my system what this does.

"Uh, Kevin, maybe you'd better keep this to yourself." I try to get up from my chair, but Kevin and André stay put. So either I leave the two of them together without me or sit back down and face this.

I sit.

In the few seconds I have to work this out before he says even more, I realize that: one, the secret's out, so I might as well receive the news as anyone else would, and two, I'll at least be witness to André's reaction before he has a chance to get himself together. And, oh, yeah, three, what's up with Essie Sue?

"What did you hear?" André asks again. "We love gossip."

"That Serena Salit may have been poisoned instead of having a heart attack."

André's face freezes halfway between a grin and a grimace. Honestly, I've never seen anyone go so white.

"How was she poisoned?" he says.

I'm not operating on all cylinders yet, but that's a very strange first question.

"They think she may have been injected. That's all Sara said."

Now it's André's idea to run. "I'm sorry," he says, "this is too upsetting. Serena was close to all of us in the quartet, you know. I have to go back to my room."

Kevin and I are left facing each other in the bedroom, and since André hasn't closed the door behind him, I take a quick peek and see that he's slipped out of Irene's suite altogether. Since I don't have the others' reactions to think about, this bedroom is probably the best place to be for a while, but I'll have to work fast.

"Okay, Kevin," I say. "What's this Essie Sue business?"

"She said it would look terrible for our choir at this conference if Serena had been poisoned at our latke party, and that she was sorry I even told her."

"I truly doubt that, Kevin — she lives for this stuff. She probably just wanted to be one of the few people who knew."

"She seemed really mad at me for saying anything. I should have waited and told you first."

"Did you tell me second, at least?"

"Yes — you and André. I wouldn't have told, except you said it was okay to talk to both of you in here."

Yeah, that was definitely brilliant of me. I shouldn't be surprised, though — Paul said this wouldn't remain a secret for long in Eternal. I know Bart Goldman learned about it from Joellyn's email, and now André's aware, too. Only Irene to go, as far as the quartet is concerned.

"André was shocked," Kevin said. "I guess it's pretty devastating news."

André could have been bowled over by the fact that the authorities found out about it, not that it happened. I agree with Kevin that he *was* devastated. But I wonder how shocked.

33

I'm relieved that we're back on track, literally. This is our last chance to see Canada
by train, and today we're scheduled to pass
through some of the most spectacular
scenery on the continent. I'm determined
not to miss it, and I know that if I keep
ruminating on the events of the early morning, I'll give up any chance of enjoying this
unbelievable landscape.

Not that it's easy to make the transition.
Once André left the bedroom this morning,
I managed to calm Kevin enough to slip us
both out of the room while the meditation
service was winding up. I'm sure Irene was
curious as to why André had left so fast,
and she probably wasted no time hunting
him down. But we left it to her to deal with
— I was personally determined to get my
morning coffee or else, and I think Kevin
just wanted to get out of there.

I *am* curious to know whether Essie Sue

decided to keep the news of Serena to herself — if so, it'll be a first. So now she knows, I do, Kevin does, and André and Bart Goldman do. And whoever else is in contact with friends or family in Eternal — making it just about unanimous, I suppose. Some open secrets, though, are more whispered about than shouted, and I suspect this is one of them. I'm guessing that if the news is being discussed, it's in confidence between one person and another, with each one thinking it's still a secret from everyone else.

I know one thing — I've got to have a break from all this. I want to help Paul despite the fact that he thinks it's too dangerous, but at the same time, I came on this trip to enjoy myself, and I've done bloody little of that. And because I love photography, I've made sure that the batteries in my camera are charged and I have plenty of room on the memory card.

The open spaces between the first few cars are still crowded with photographers from our choir groups, and I can see that if I take too many photos this way, I'm likely to have someone's shoulder or elbow sticking smack in the middle of my picture. There's got to be another option.

My first goal is to avoid a lot of time-wasting conversation while I'm searching out good camera angles, and the best way to do that is not to hang out in cars full of Temple Rita congregants. I head back to the end of the train, many cabins away from our group, with tourists who aren't even a part of the choir convention. It seems to take ages to get back there, but it's worth it. And yay, nobody knows me. There's a big observation car near the end of the train that's perfect — the windows are huge, kept sparkling clean by the maintenance staff.

The best thing about my digital camera is the playback feature, and I can always see if my photos are correctly exposed and composed before wasting more time and effort. I take several test photos to see if the reflection from the windows will be a problem, but if I angle the shots right and photograph straight through the glass, I'm good to go. And of course, since I'm never more content than when I'm happily snapping pictures of great scenery, I'm in pixel heaven.

I get some great shots as we're crossing Eagle River Bridge, where salmon spawn in the fall. The scenery's marked by milepost signs, so we know how far we've traveled. The Adams River sockeye salmon run is huge, although no one really knows how the fish navigate. The guides tell us it's by smell or magnetic orientation, but whatever, this is where romance among the sockeyes happens. The female opens her mouth and discharges a stream of eggs from her vent, while the male, close to the stream, releases the milt that fertilizes the eggs. Since I consider salmon to be food from the gods, I definitely want to document the breeding grounds.

I'm snapping like mad when I turn too far sideways to avoid the reflection from the window — not good. And I see something I'm not expecting reflected in the glass — it's the face of someone wearing a blue, denimlike baseball cap pulled down over his or her head, with brown hair going down a couple inches from the hat. Not long hair — more like a short haircut that's getting too long and needs a trim.

I immediately try to sit straight ahead and correct my viewing angle through the camera lens so I won't get a reflection, but then I turn — just a reflex action, I think — and look around to see whose face that was. I don't see anyone and I hear people in the observation car *ooh*ing and *aah*ing over a quick view of Kay Falls, a waterfall that runs down Mount Griffin. It's one of those sights you can miss if you're not fast, so I take a few rapid shots in the general direction. I don't have time to zoom, so I'm sure they won't be any good, but with a digital camera, who cares? Later, I can just delete the ones I don't like.

I take a rest when the attendant comes through the car with a basket of fruit for a late-morning treat. I recognize her from yesterday's trip — she's a pleasant person.

"How's it going?" she says. "Are you getting some prizewinning snapshots?"

"Well, you certainly can't beat the subject matter," I say, helping myself to an apple. "Whether my talent can match it is another story. But I'm having fun."

"That's the idea," she says.

She's getting ready to move on when I blurt out something I didn't even know I was going to say.

"Hey," I say, "did you run into someone in the aisle just a couple of minutes ago? Wearing a baseball cap? The face looked vaguely familiar, but then when I looked around, there was no one there."

She shakes her head no, gives me a nice smile, and moves on.

None of this is exactly unusual, except that I didn't realize until I spoke to the attendant that this was a face I knew.

34

Lunch is on the way already, so I go forward several cars — I take a minute to look around for a baseball cap, but people aren't choosing to wear hats of any kind inside the train. I don't waste time on my search — heaven forbid that I should miss a meal, and we have to be in our seats to be served. Today it's smoked salmon salad or turkey sandwiches, and of course I pick the salmon. When in Rome, et cetera, and after all, we're not rolling through turkey-breeding country out these windows. Plum tomatoes and some really good homemade chips are piled on the plate along with the salad greens. I'm glad I didn't finish my apple earlier.

"I'm joining you, Ruby."

It's Essie Sue, of course — she's the only one I know who wouldn't ask "*May* I join you?" and she plops down beside me with her lunch tray. She's having turkey.

"Too much salmon," she says. "That's all

they seem to eat up here, and who knows where it's been? I'm watching my mercury."

Well, we can see where it's been, but I don't bother to point that out, or to mention the questionable poultry processing her sandwich might have gone through on its way here. I use the word *sandwich* loosely — since, of course, she only eats the middle of things. I haven't seen her down a piece of bread since I've known her. I think of asking for her brownie, which I know will remain on her tray, destined for the garbage, but that's only a fleeting, random thought. I haven't lost my mind yet, and I have enough trouble reaching for my own brownie, knowing she'll have something to say about it.

"You're not eating that brownie, are you?" she says.

"Looks like it," I say.

"It has fat calories — the worst kind," she says. "And when fat is married to sugar —"

"I know," I say, "Lucifer's spawn. I'm damned."

"Why do you think they call it devil's food cake?" she says.

I actually don't know the answer to that, but I do know that I'm devoutly wishing she hadn't come along to ruin my delicious lunch. I wish there were a special sort of hell for these people, but they'd probably get off on the deprivation.

She watches me choke down the rest of my lunch, and then leans closer to me.

"Ruby, I have to ask you something," she says.

"Hurry up," I say, "because I'm only staying while lunch is served. When the coffee comes around, I'm outta here."

"Where's to go?" she says. "It's all the same train. Have you seen André Korman? We were going to have an informal meeting, but I can't find him."

This happens a lot to Essie Sue, I notice — people disappear on her whenever they get the chance.

"I haven't seen him," I say. "Is that what you wanted to ask me?"

"No," she says, "I had something more important to talk about."

"Here's the coffee guy," I say. "You have ten minutes while I drink some."

I would have said five minutes, but I'm thinking she's going to pump me about what Paul's told me regarding Serena Salit's death, and I'm curious to hear her take on all this.

"Did the rabbi say anything to you about a conversation he had with someone back home in Eternal? He heard some gossip."

"You know the rabbi doesn't gossip," I say

demurely. I'm going to make her do the gossiping herself.

"Well, they say Serena didn't have a heart attack — she was poisoned."

"Really?"

She cocks her head at me. "You always know everything, Ruby. Don't tell me you weren't aware of this. You said yourself that you speak to Paul on the phone all the time."

"I said nothing of the sort," I say. "He just happened to call the other night when we were together, and you got it out of me that he was the one on the telephone. It wasn't a business call."

"So why aren't you surprised?" she says. "You did know, didn't you?"

"I'd heard some stray remarks, too," I say. "But until we get back home, you might as well realize that we won't have the whole story. Why waste time with it up here?"

I knew she'd ignore me, and she does. "Who could have done it?" she says.

"I didn't know her that well, Essie Sue," I say truthfully. "How could I even guess? And anyway, isn't that the job of the police?"

"It's a *shandah* for the temple," she says. "A disgrace."

"I don't need a translation," I say. "You mean because she was poisoned at the temple?"

"That, and because all her friends were temple people. That's who probably murdered her."

"Who? Neither of us has any idea who all her friends were, Essie Sue. Is this all you're going on?"

"Not exactly."

I'm drinking my coffee more slowly now. I might as well hear her out.

"So what?" I say. "Get to the point."

"It's just that I heard her divorce wasn't all that kosher," she says. "What I found out at the time was that either she or Bart was carrying on with someone. Or maybe both were."

"Maybe? So you really don't know anything," I say.

"It's something for the police to look into," she says. "And I intend to tell them. Unless you want to tell your boyfriend now instead of waiting until we get back to Eternal."

"If you think it's so important, why don't you tell him?" I say. "But he's certainly going to grill you about what else you might know. From what I can see, this is pure speculation."

"A lot of people thought Bart was running around," she says. "Or that she was."

"So name them," I say. "Let's get to the bottom of it. All I can see now is that you don't even know which of them was cheating on the marriage — that's not exactly cogent documentation."

"I got my information from his receptionist," Essie Sue says. "The one he fired two months ago."

"So much for the temple members," I say. "And a discharged employee — that's a real find. But do pass it along if you want to."

"I want you to do it," she says, "because as I told the rabbi, this could look very bad for Temple Rita — especially at the start of our new building project."

I haven't heard of the umpteenth new building project, and I frankly don't want to know.

"Call Paul if you want to," I say — a throwaway line if I ever heard one. She's going to do exactly what she pleases whether I give her my permission or not, and it's not as though I own Paul Lundy.

I make sure I have my camera with me, and I'm stepping out into the aisle when I glimpse Gus Goren in between cars.

"Gotta go, Essie Sue," I say. "I've got to see some people."

I don't mention Gus — there's no way I want her noodging me about him.

"When will you be back?" she says. "I only see you when you're sleepy."

"Later," I say, making my way through the car as fast as possible without doing anything that might induce her to follow me.

"Hey, Gus," I say when I catch up with him.

"Ruby." He seems genuinely glad to see me, and gives me that smile I haven't forgotten.

"Where have you been, girl?" he says. "I've looked all over for you since our little bus ride."

"Attending too many meetings and dodging too many people," I tell him. "I'm finally taking some time to get more pictures of this gorgeous scenery. Are you a photo bug, too? If so, you're welcome to come with me."

He pulls out a tiny camera similar to my own. "Shirt pocket variety," he says, "but it takes great snapshots."

"Mine's a mini, too," I say, "that way, I always have it with me. No camera bags needed."

"Where are you headed?" he says.

"To the caboose," I say, "if they have one. I want to hang out on the very back end of the train, where I can have swivel room. My only concern is that it might be crowded.

Wanna give it a try?"

"Sure. Let's go."

The train's flying as we scoot through the cars, and I have to hold on to keep from being thrown around. Of course, Gus'd be there to catch me, right? But I'm not quite ready to try that approach.

"What's the hurry?" he says. "You're a hard woman to keep up with."

"I just want to make sure the afternoon light's good," I say. "Or maybe I'm so used to being distracted from the things I really want to do on this trip that I don't want to take the chance of being cornered by anyone."

"So that doesn't include me, huh?" he says. "I guess I should be complimented."

"It definitely doesn't include you," I say. "You're fun to be with."

He actually does steady me a couple of times when the train lurches around a curve, and I have to admit, it's nice.

I'm glad I've worn my wool sweater as we approach the outside rails of the last car. There's a brisk breeze out here, and I even have to jam on the stocking cap I knitted last fall so my ears won't get cold.

"Don't cover up all the curls," he says. "I like them."

"Yeah, I can imagine what I look like in

this stretchy wool hat," I say, "but nothing keeps me warmer, so that's the way it is."

"I was kidding about the curls," he says. "If it's cold, it's cold. Besides, you look cute in that hat."

"Good," I say. "That's a bonus."

There are a couple of other people out here, but not a crowd. The cold wind has probably scared the hordes away, because this is definitely the best spot on the train for picture taking. With the wind blowing, though, and with the cap over my ears, I can't easily hear what Gus is saying — not great for getting to know him. But he doesn't seem bothered by the lack of conversation, and he's snapping away on his own. I like this guy's style.

And what a time to be out here — we're not too far from the Continental Divide, and we're traveling in and out of the famous Spiral Tunnels. When the railroad was first built in the early 1900s, there was a dangerous grade called the Big Hill by the engineers. Two spiral tunnels were constructed to lower the grade so that a fast-moving train could navigate the terrain safely.

"These things were modeled after gorge tunnels in Switzerland," Gus yells at me through the wind. "It took a thousand men to build them, but they reduced the grade to a safe level."

The Lower Spiral tunnels its way through Mount Ogden, and the Upper travels through Cathedral Mountain. Each tunnel emerges many feet higher than its entrance, so that the railway doubles back on itself twice to cut down the grade — it turns out to be an *amazing* maze.

We're coming out of the Upper Spiral near milepost 128, and I'm focusing on an especially beautiful spot where we've crossed the river for the second time in that doubling-back process. Because we're the last car of the train, we have a fabulous, unrestricted view.

I have to blink my eyes to make sure they're not blurring, but I distinctly see a human form lying on the riverbank as we pass. I yell, but Gus doesn't hear me, and I pull on his arm.

"Look — over there on the bank."

"An otter?" he asks. He points in that direction so that the other two people on the platform with us can see, too.

"No, a person. I saw a person," I scream at him.

It's obvious that none of the others saw what I saw, and I snap more photos as we roar past the scene. I also make a note of the milepost number I noticed back there — 128.

I pull on Gus again until he comes back inside the last car with me.

"Hey, you're upset," he says. "I didn't realize — I'm sorry. Tell me again what you saw."

We sit down in two empty seats at the end of the car and he gently pulls off my hat for me.

"So you can hear me," he says. "What happened, Ruby?"

35

"There was someone on the curve of the riverbank," I say, "not far from the tunnel we just came through. The person was facedown, with one leg skewed at a peculiar angle."

"Could they have been camping or fishing?" Gus says.

"Maybe to begin with," I say, "but I'm positive that body looked hurt, if not worse."

"Was it a man? Did you see anything alongside it?"

"I have no idea if it was a man or a woman, Gus. I just know I saw it. Let's go back outside and check with the other two people."

"They came in after we did, Ruby, and they left. I have no idea who they were — I was too busy worrying about you. You scared me. But I do know we all shrugged when you said you saw someone — I don't think they caught it any more than I did."

"They didn't," I say. "I could tell. I guess I'm the only one."

"So now what?" he says. "You know what they say about this backcountry that the train cuts through — it's only accessible to hikers. The train passengers get great views, but otherwise, not even the dirt roads reach it, much less the highways."

"I have to speak to a conductor," I say. "Can you bring one here? I don't want to go back through all those cars filled with curious people — especially a bunch of folks I know. Not until I've nailed this down."

"Sure," he says, "although the two folks outside with us didn't seem that curious, so I'm not certain you're right about everyone possibly being so concerned when you tell them."

"How about you?" I say. "You don't think I made this up, do you?"

"Of course not," he says. "But what you observed could have lots of explanations. We were going fast, for one thing, so nothing's that clear. I'm still thinking it could have been a fisherman stretched out for a nap, or reaching for something. And if it is more drastic, how would you find them, anyway?"

"That's what the railroad personnel can tell us," I say.

Gus puts his arms around me in a quick bear hug, then stands up.

"Can I get you some water first?" he says. "Or anything else?"

"Thanks for understanding," I say, shaking my head no to the water.

"I won't be long," he says.

I lay my head back on the seat, take some deep breaths, and try to calm down while he's gone. But I have a really bad feeling about this. I just wish it hadn't happened so fast.

"Ruby, this is the conductor."

I've barely closed my eyes before Gus returns with an older man in uniform. He wears glasses and has a potbelly like something out of the movies — all that's missing is the watch and chain lying on his stomach.

"Miss, I'm Charles Strong. I understand you're reporting an accident you viewed as we were coming out of the tunnel?"

His matter-of-fact acceptance makes me feel better. Gus must have done a good job of giving him the details — such as they are. That makes me feel better about Gus, too. At least he didn't doubt me.

I tell Charles Strong what I saw and ask him what he can do about it.

"Sometimes we can check out these things," he says, "and sometimes not. It's hard to get back there in the wilderness, especially when we don't know where *there* is. 'Coming out of the tunnel' is not the same as having precise directions."

"But I do know where it is," I say. "It was right at milepost 128."

"You have the number?" he says. "Are you sure?"

"Yes, I've been photographing certain mileposts near scenes I want to keep track of, just in case I want to identify something later. I noticed that your guidebook lists mileposts, and I thought it would be a big help."

He writes down my information in his notebook.

"So can't you call this in now?" I say. "Certainly the police would want to know."

"I'll let them know," he says, "but don't assume they'll do anything about it right away — they have their priorities."

"But why can't the next train through here be on the lookout for the body, or whatever it was?" I say. "And certainly, if someone is wounded, we need to find him. Or her. When's the next train?"

"In a couple of hours," he says.

"Then follow your routine with the police report," I say, "but do me a favor — call the engineer of the next train and ask that he slow down at that milepost. Surely you can do that."

The conductor looks at Gus. "Your lady sure is strong-willed," he says.

"Well, she's not my lady, but I've seen firsthand that she's quite determined," Gus says. "If I were you, I'd give the next train a call. If you don't, it'll be too dark to do anything until tomorrow morning."

"And by then," I say, "an animal could disturb the scene, or do worse if the person is alive."

"I don't think you have any idea," the conductor says, "how difficult it is to get a railroad to go off schedule. It's not what they want to hear."

"Please," I say. "You can't tell me there aren't ways to cooperate between the lines here. Do you know the personnel on the next train?"

"As a matter of fact, I do," he says, "and that's the only reason I'm giving you any encouragement. I've been on this line for a long time now, and my buddy's operating the other train. We're meeting for dinner tonight."

"Could you call him for us off the record?" Gus says.

"All right, I'll call his cell phone," Mr. Strong says. "But we'll be well past Banff before he gets a chance to look. You'll be off the train by then. You're with the big group that's getting off there, aren't you?"

"Yes, but that's okay," I say. "I just couldn't live with myself knowing nothing was being done. It could have been a camper having a medical problem, or who knows what else."

"We appreciate the heads-up," he says. "And we respect our passengers. Thank you both."

He starts down the aisle, when I stand up and touch his arm.

"Mr. Strong," I say, "could you please make the call now? I know how many distractions you can face once you go back through those cars."

Gus gets up, too, to my great relief.

"Why not have it behind you?" he says to Mr. Strong. "Then you won't have to look over your shoulder to find this lady following you. Or having you paged."

"You're a persuasive pair when you gang up on a fellow," he says, sitting down beside us. "But I do have a request of you both. Rumors multiply like flies inside the confined space of a train — especially if groups are traveling together. I'm asking you not to speak about this to anyone else until we verify something one way or another. It's a policy the railroad follows if at all possible. Have you spoken to anyone yet?"

"Well," I say, "those other two people were outside the last car with us when I first saw something, but they didn't seem very interested — I think they assumed I'd seen a person fishing. They went in shortly after, and Gus and I had no way of knowing who they were."

"Nothing we can do about that, then," Mr. Strong says. "But no one in your group has been told?"

"We're with people from different states here for a conference," Gus says, "and we haven't run into anyone — we've been busy reporting to you."

Mr. Strong seems satisfied, and makes the call to the next train. He asks his friend to watch out for a hiker or fisherman down at milepost 128, and then hangs up.

"Will you do me a big favor and take my cell phone number?" I say. "If you have any news of the hiker or whoever it is, will you give me a call? I just want to know the person's okay."

"I can do that," he says. He shakes our hands and leaves, taking my number and the name of my hotel in Banff with him.

I put an arm around Gus and give him a quick half-hug.

"You're the man," I say. "Really, I couldn't be more appreciative. Without you, he might have thought I was just another hysterical woman. This conductor seemed to be a fair-minded person, but who knows what he would have done without your input? I was pretty excited."

"Ha." Gus laughs at me. "I don't believe for a minute that you couldn't have over-whelmed this guy on your own, Ruby. But I'm glad I'm appreciated, anyway."

"How about dinner when we get to Banf?" I say. "On me."

"I most definitely accept," he says. "We'll fight over the check later."

36

Gus and I find our separate seats for the rest of the trip to Banff. I want to relax, and Gus is meeting some friends in his part of the train. He invited me along, but I needed to calm down. I'm not in the mood to make conversation with strangers, and I can still look forward to seeing him for dinner tonight.

I slide into my window space, lean my head back, and close my eyes for a few minutes. At least, I think it's only a few minutes. The next thing I feel is Kevin punching my shoulder.

"Ouch. What are you doing?" I say.

"I'm nudging you awake," he says.

"That's not a nudge, Kevin, it's a hit. I'll probably have a bruise there. Haven't you heard of communicating with speech?"

"I tried that. You didn't wake up."

"I'm definitely awake now. What do you want?"

"Essie Sue sent me to find you and bring you to the club car — we're having a meeting there before we get off the train and go to the hotel. It's for that executive committee she set up."

Nobody told me I was on an executive committee, but that's no surprise. I don't bother protesting — she'll just come herself if Kevin doesn't fetch me. And I'd rather meet now than be disturbed later tonight when I'm having dinner.

"What's on tap for tonight?" I say.

"I have no idea," he says. "You know I'm always the last to find out stuff. Probably some sort of planning for the ChoirFest tomorrow."

"Well, whatever it is tonight, I can't come."

Being Kevin, he's not curious, but that doesn't mean Essie Sue and the rest of them won't be. I'm wondering whether it'll be easier just to say I'm meeting Gus or be evasive. Straightforward is probably better with this crowd. If I'm cutesy about it, they'll be all over me. At least we're meeting in the club car, where they're serving drinks — maybe they'll be feeling no pain by the time I join them. And I can sure use a glass of wine or stronger.

Stronger it is — by the time I get back

there, everyone's ordering whiskey sours — I haven't had one of those in years. The club car is filled with partiers, and the spirit is apparently infecting our little Eternal group meeting in one corner.

"Oh, you found her," Essie Sue says to Kevin by way of a greeting.

"Hello to you, too," I say. "I'll take one of those sours you're all having. Why *sours*, by the way?"

"Because they're made with Canadian whiskey," Essie Sue says. "We wanted to do as the natives do, and everyone started copying us."

I'm not sure the indigenous peoples would agree, but who am I to question such quaint practices, especially when backed by the expertise coming from our own natives of Eternal, Texas?

Bart and Irene have obviously had a few. It's always hard to tell what Essie Sue's been on, since she's so often high from her own narcissism. At any rate, maybe the meeting won't be so dull this way.

"Why didn't you find André?" Irene asks Kevin. "Weren't you supposed to?"

"André doesn't need finding," Essie Sue says, "he's much more responsible than Ruby. He'll find us rather than the other way around."

"Thanks for the backhanded compliment," I say.

"Oh, it wasn't a compliment, Ruby."

Imagine that.

"Maybe André's found a better way to spend the cocktail hour," I say. "Why don't we forget about the meeting and relax like everyone else?"

"No, we have to plan our strategy for the vocal contest taking place in two days," Essie Sue says. "My idea is to pass out flyers at the conference advertising how good our singers are. We should definitely put them in the restrooms — no one can miss them there. It's a unique approach to influencing the judges."

"Unique and classy — don't forget that," I remind her. "But only if the judges are having the travel trots, right?"

"Do you have a better idea, Ruby?" Irene asks.

"Not really. Let's vote on it and adjourn."

"I concur," Kevin says. "I have to meet Bitsy. She felt left out that you didn't invite her to the meeting."

"She's on a subcommittee," Essie Sue says. "She'll get her chance. Maybe she's with André."

Kevin obviously doesn't like that. If he were anyone else, I'd say his jaw just fell, but Kevin's jaw usually clenches in these situations. He gives me a helpless look.

"Why don't you go look for her?" I say. "I doubt she's with André. And this is a short meeting, isn't it, Essie Sue?"

"Well, since you all adopted my idea so readily, I suppose this part of the meeting is over," she says. "I'm assigning the task of producing the flyers to you, Irene. I'm sure you'll do a sterling job. Make them that popular color of chartreuse they're showing."

"That'll do worlds for the people in the bathrooms," I say. "If they're not nauseous when they come in, they will be before they come out. How about something more neutral?"

"Neutral is boring, Ruby. This premeeting is adjourned."

I don't mind at all being spurned, as long as I can get out of here.

"Ruby and Rabbi," Essie Sue says, "why are you leaving?"

"Because you said so," Kevin says.

"I only said this part was over," she says. "We're all joining the Eternal contingent in our regular car for a bus check. It's mandatory."

"Says who?" I say.

"All the groups are doing it," Essie Sue

274

says. "We have announcements to make, room reservations to go over, ChoirFest schedule changes to hand out, and a question-and-answer session before we get on the buses. The planners decided it would be impossible to keep up with everyone once we arrive in Banff."

I can't argue with her — it does seem more practical. "But we're free once we get there, yes?" I ask.

"That's why we're having this meeting now," she says, "so we'll be finished. Unless you and I need to get together . . ."

"No way," I say. "I'm finished, too, for the evening. Don't wait up."

I jump up to lead the way back to our car before my last remark becomes provocative. It looks as if everyone has gotten the word, because a rambunctious bunch of Temple Rita congregants greet us. I'm sure they're all as restless as I am, despite the beauty of the train trip.

Essie Sue's in charge, of course, and I must say she's conducting the proceedings with dispatch. She makes the announcements and passes out the papers without the usual digressions.

"How about a closing prayer, Rabbi?" she says when her checklist is completed.

"Huh?" he says. "What's *closing* about this?"

"The end of the train trip."

"Can we have music first?" he says. The word *extemporaneous* is not part of Kevin's vocabulary, and he's angling for time.

"We can't," Irene says. "André's not here."

"He has to be," Essie Sue says. "We're doing a final count."

"Well, he isn't," Irene says.

"I already looked for him on the way here," Bart says to Essie Sue. "I gave his name to an attendant and they'll ask around for him."

"Well, we need him if we're having any music," she says. "He always leads. And we'll be pulling into Banff soon."

Kevin nudges me. "His backpack's on the floor under his seat," he says.

"Give it to me," I say. He kicks it along toward my seat and I put it with my own pack and my coat. I'm not quite sure yet why I want to keep this myself instead of letting someone else carry it, but I do. It's a miracle Kevin hasn't blurted this out, but I'm counting my blessings.

"Let's go to the bathroom," I say.

"I don't have to go," Kevin says. "And I have to make up a prayer."

"Just come for a minute and stay close to

me," I say. "I'll keep this for André and I'll help you with the closing prayer, too."

"We're using the restroom while you're finding André," I tell Essie Sue as we get up. "We'll be back in a minute for the prayer."

"I'm canceling the prayer," she says. "We don't have a lot of time, and it won't be spiritual without the music. Everyone, get your things together."

Only Essie Sue and God can cancel prayers, I think, in that order. But whatever the sequence, Kevin seems relieved as we leave the car.

"You passed the bathroom back there," he says.

"I don't have to go," I say. "I wanted to save this for André without calling attention to it."

"Why?"

The train comes lurching to a stop before I have to answer, and since we're between cars, we're the first ones off. I see a couple of policemen at the station — maybe the conductor's called them.

I get Kevin to help me put all our stuff on the bus between our two seats. It's a short ride to the hotel, but it's dark and we can't really see the beautiful Banff I've heard about. Essie Sue gives André's name to the bus driver in case he appears. I'm very curious as to why he hasn't shown up — it's not that simple to get lost on a train, and I have an uneasy feeling about this. At least the bus and train people have his name.

"I've made all the announcements," Essie Sue says, "so our Temple Rita people should be totally caught up with what's going on. We're all accounted for except for one, and I'm sure he's probably on one of the other buses. And just to double-check again, has anyone seen André Korman this afternoon?"

I certainly hope I haven't.

37

Our hotel has a rustic flavor — beamed ceilings in the lobby and a huge fireplace. Kevin and I are standing in line to register, which gives me time to decide how I want to handle the matter of the extra backpack I'm carrying. No problem when André shows up — I can get points for keeping it safe for him. Our larger baggage is handled by the tour people — that'll be taken directly to our rooms. At the moment, though, I just don't want to unload his backpack in my own place if there's any chance my roommate might be there.

I decide that Kevin's room would be ideal — he's rooming with André, so it'll be perfectly natural if the backpack's there when André returns.

"Kevin, let's keep this in your room for André, okay? I'll take it up with you."

"Whatever you want to do, Ruby."

He's already lost interest, I can tell. We're

next to register, and it doesn't take much time.

"There's Bitsy," I say, "standing in the last line on the right."

"Finally," he says. "I keep missing her. We have plans for dinner, and I need to talk to her."

"Give me your key," I say, "and I'll take this to your room while you go over there."

He hands me the key card. I separate it from my own and get on the elevator before the crowd. I don't see Essie Sue, which is a relief.

I open the door to Kevin's room and don't even bother to turn on the lamps. The curtain's open, and the lights from the hotel entrance below cast a glow back through the window. I'm suddenly tired, but before I do anything else, I put the backpack on the floor of the closet. Then I lay back on one of the double beds and stare at the dark sky outside.

When my cell phone rings, the sound seems to be drifting from another planet. It rings a few times before it hits me that I'm supposed to answer — my brain is foggy and I realize I've zonked out for who knows how long.

"Hello," I answer.

"Miss, this is Mr. Strong, the conductor

you spoke to on the train. I'm about to go off duty, but I remembered you asked me to call."

"Yes, thanks so much for doing that. Did the other train pass the milepost before it got too dark to see anything?"

"It did. And I'm sorry to say that a body was seen at the place you indicated. It had likely fallen from a great height — either from the banks up by the train tracks or possibly from the train itself. That's all I know. But my supervisors had me give them the note you left with me — your phone number and the name of your hotel. Someone will be contacting you and your friend for more information, I'm sure."

I'm not groggy anymore, but what he's saying is not quite real, either.

"I have to go, miss," he says, "there's nothing else I know."

"Do you know if it was a man or a woman?" I ask.

"I believe it was a man."

Oh boy. I thank him for calling, fling myself back on the bed, and stare at the ceiling. I think of that man lying down there alone.

I know someone in authority will be calling any minute, and I have a sudden urge to call Paul before they do — he can get me to the right people and save a lot of time. Besides, I just need to hear his voice.

There's a knock on the door, and in my spaced-out state, I'm thinking they've already located me.

"Ruby, open up. It's Kevin."

I forgot that I'm not in my own room. I open the door and he comes in with his big duffel bag as well as his train case.

"I thought I'd bring my bag up before waiting for them to deliver it," he says. In my still-spaced-out state, I can't think of much to say, or that I should say, for that matter, so I ask to use his bathroom, which is fast becoming a necessity, anyway.

When I come out, Kevin's duffel has been put away in the closet, and he's sitting on one of the beds with André's backpack open in his lap.

"Essie Sue asked me to look in this," he says. "André has all the notes and directions for our choir presentation tomorrow, and she can't wait until he shows up to get them. In fact, she's making preparations for Irene to take over, if necessary, and Irene needs his stuff now. I want to hurry so I can go out to dinner with Bitsy."

He dumps the contents of the center compartment onto the bed before I can stop him. And the truth is that I don't know what

I could say *to* stop him without revealing a lot more than I want to at the moment. I've got to talk to Paul.

"Here's some stuff that looks musical," he says, pulling out a spiral notebook — it says *Choir.* "And here's a handwritten letter and some other stuff. Should I give her this, or the whole backpack?"

I can't answer, because I'm staring at a syringe that's rolling out on the bed — not musical but certainly private. Suddenly I know I have to do something before he goes any further.

"Kevin, André hasn't come to the room yet, and I think you should put these things back for when he does. We were just safe-guarding it for him."

"No, Essie Sue said to look. And you know how she is when she needs something. He's not going to care, Ruby."

Yeah, I already thought of that.

I'm about to tell him to take the choir notebook so Essie Sue won't come to the room and search for herself, when he looks at the letter he found. I've never seen Kevin blush, believe it or not, but he's blushing now. He's a bit nearsighted, and he holds the paper close to his face while he concentrates. Frankly, I've never seen him focus all this much, either. I know I should stop him, but he's probably halfway through it already, and my natural curiosity's taking over. So I wait.

He's still reading, but he comes up for air. "Wow," he says, and dives back in.

"So what's in it?" I say. I've never been too good at restraining myself. And I keep thinking that if I were the one who was reading this stuff, I might be doing something wrong, like tampering with evidence, knowing what I know. Or to be more accurate, guessing what I'm guessing.

The weird thing is that I can't really tell myself that the body I saw down at the river was André. I certainly don't know that yet, and there could be a thousand more explanations. Except, of course, that he hasn't turned up.

Kevin puts down the letter and takes off his glasses to wipe them.

"They're steamy," he says, suppressing a smile, which immediately turns into a frown. "André's gonna kill me. You won't tell him I read this, will you, Ruby?"

"Not if you give me a total description of it right this minute," I say, figuring the odds are good I won't be telling André.

"It's a passionate love letter he wrote," he says. "I heard this guy was hot with women, but this is amazing. If I could use some of

284

this with my online dates, I'll bet they'd be flocking to me."

"Who's it written to?" I say.

"That's the peculiar part," he says. "I don't know why he has it — maybe he didn't send it, or he sent a copy of it."

"Or maybe he's getting ready to send it," I say.

"Well, if that's the case, then he's a little late," Kevin says. "The love letter is written to Serena Salit."

"So wait a minute," I say. "You're telling me there's a letter from André to Serena in André's backpack? She's been dead for a while now. Why would Serena have given it back to him, and why would he bring it to Canada with him?"

"I don't know, Ruby, and besides, I have to get back to Essie Sue — she said to meet her in the lobby with André's choir directions."

"I wish you hadn't told her we had his backpack," I say.

"You know how she sees right through me," he says. "But do you think I need to give her the other stuff I found?"

"Absolutely not, Kevin. Put it away in the backpack and leave it in the closet until I can speak to Paul."

We're on our way out of Kevin's room

when his phone rings — so loud that it makes me jump.

"It's probably Essie Sue," he says, "wondering why I'm late. Tell her I'm on my way down."

"Oh, no," I say. "You get it. She doesn't need to know I'm anywhere near here."

He stays on the phone for a decidedly one-sided conversation that doesn't seem as if it will ever end. By the time he sits down on one of the beds to listen to the caller with a glazed look on his face, I'm convinced it's not Essie Sue.

"But why are you asking me?" he finally says. "Can you hold on for a minute?"

He covers the mouthpiece and I can see his hand trembling.

"Ruby, it's the Banff police calling. They have some identification on a body they found, and they want me to come down and confirm who it is. I can't quite believe this, but they think it's André Korman. Why are they calling me?"

He's not the only one who has to sit down. I grab for the other bed when I feel my knees buckling a bit.

"It's probably because you're clergy," I say. "Ask them."

He does and it is.

"Yeah," he says, "they say they heard I was

with the group, and felt I'd be the appropri-
ate person to come down, since they weren't
sure if a next of kin was aboard. They're
sending someone to the room now to escort
me."

38

I'm glad I had the presence of mind to leave the room before Kevin could rouse himself and ask me to go along. I think we were both in shock, but I had more warning than he did. And I didn't want to have to explain to him just yet about my promise to the conductor not to say anything. I'm sure I'll be interviewed soon enough, and I want to talk to Paul first.

If I could just be sure Essie Sue's not in our room, I could go up and have the place to myself for a blessed few minutes. Double-locking the door will ensure she doesn't burst in on me while I'm on the phone. I know she was supposed to meet Kevin in the lobby, so I take the elevator from his floor up to mine, avoiding her altogether, I only hope. I'm feeling relieved, too, that Kevin's the one who opened André's backpack and not me. I'm sure he'll fill the cops in on all of it, and with the extra respect he's accorded, he'll be able to handle it if he doesn't panic.

Luckily, I don't run into Essie Sue, but I do see some of the choir members in the elevator.

"Did you hear about André Korman?" Cindy Eppsman asks. "He's missing. They looked all over the train and checked the buses, and they couldn't find him."

"Yeah," her husband says, "and he never checked into his hotel room. I even heard they looked into the airline database to see if he'd returned to Eternal without telling anyone, with no results. They were thinking maybe he got some emergency call from his wife back home."

I'm glad they get off at the floor before mine so that I can look surprised but don't have to answer. Gossip being what it is, I'm not shocked that the news has spread, but apparently no one knows anything worse yet. I'm wondering if our group will even stay at the ChoirFest if it turns out that the body I saw was conclusively André.

If they're verifying that André didn't go back to Eternal, they'll obviously call his wife first. I wonder if Paul will be brought in. Regardless, he'll be upset with me if I don't fill him in on everything soon.

I hold my breath as I open the door to the

room, but as I expected, Essie Sue's not here. I lock the door, take off my shoes, fluff the pillows, and sit on my bed to relax for a minute, but not for long. The red light on the phone is flashing, and my curiosity outweighs my fatigue.

The message is from Gus, and he wants to meet me for dinner in an hour. That gives me practically no time to catch Paul before he leaves work, then shower and look half-way presentable for our — what? Is it a din-ner date with Gus? A date at all? And do I want it to be?

Oy — since Gus knows about the events of the afternoon and was so supportive and helpful, I'm feeling I should at least call and alert him of the latest before I phone Paul. Why am I letting this simple decision turn into some sort of contest between the two of them?

If it is, then Paul wins, since I pick up my cell and dial his number. I'm not sure if I'm choosing him because I know how mad he'll be if I don't tell him fast, or because I'm afraid he'll call *me* when I'm out with Gus tonight.

One thing I do know — Gus can wait an hour to hear about André, and I need to contact Paul before the police interview me. We haven't phoned on this trip as much as

I'd expected. Paul doesn't seem to be calling me all that often, and I'm not reaching for the telephone that much, either, so I guess we're both somewhat at fault.

"Ruby. It's good to hear from you. I was just about to go home. What's up there in Canada?"

I think I can safely assume he hasn't heard anything about André being missing — he wouldn't have started off that way.

"Good to hear your voice, too," I say. Of course, he didn't say it was good to hear my voice, just that it was good to hear from me — there's a difference. I mentally slap myself for being such a trivial idiot, and get to the point.

"I hardly know where to begin," I say, and then find a way to describe all the events of the afternoon while not saying much about the fact that Gus was experiencing the whole thing with me.

The most surprising thing is that I'm fighting back tears the whole time I'm talking to Paul.

"I'm sorry," I say. "I guess the day was more stressful and emotional than I've been willing to admit. If I'd given in to it earlier, I'm not certain I would have been able to get through everything."

"You mean seeing a body and then learning it was someone you knew? I'd say that would throw anyone, Ruby. None of this has filtered back down here to Eternal — or at least not to the police. But surely someone will notify Sara Korman of her husband's death as soon as the rabbi identifies the body. Is there a chance it's not André?"

"I doubt it — they said there was identification on him. Do you think he threw himself off the train, or could he have fallen while he was taking pictures or something? I don't see him as being the suicidal type — not that it's that easy to tell."

"There's a third alternative, Ruby. André could have been pushed."

39

Paul wants me back right away — no surprise there. And after I tell him that a love letter to Serena was found in André's backpack along with a syringe, he's even more adamant.

"Serena's death was caused by an injection, Ruby. A murderer could have been loose on that train. I want you out of there."

"If you're talking murderers, Paul, maybe André killed Serena. The syringe was found in his own backpack, remember — if its presence doesn't have some more innocent explanation. We're not in the enclosed space of a train right now, so I can't see that my safety's compromised. Not any more than that of the other choir members. I'm thinking that if André was as in love with Serena as that letter indicated, and then was driven by some unknown circumstance to kill her, suicide's looking a lot more probable, right?"

"It'd be great if you'd leave the speculation to the police," he says, "not that you've
ever done that before. Which reminds me
— they won't have much chance of seeing
the whole picture if you don't turn in that
backpack to them right away."

"I figured they'd search his hotel room as
soon as Kevin identifies the body," I say. "I
think it's better if I stay out of it."

"If they don't search the room by the end
of the evening, then either you or the rabbi
should tell them it's there," Paul says. "One
more time, though — did you see anyone or
anything suspicious on the train this afternoon?"

I tell him about the fleeting glance I had
earlier of the face in the baseball cap, but I
can't think of anything else. And since that
happened so fast it was almost ethereal, it's
not too helpful. The only thing I can compare it to is something you see in a dream,
but that's lost as soon as you awake.

"Someone's knocking on my door, Paul,"
I say, not mentioning that it's probably Gus.
"Can I call you back later tonight or tomorrow morning? I'm sure I'll know lots more
when Kevin gets back."

I'm glad the conversation didn't have a
chance to get personal. Although Paul
knows I haven't wanted an exclusive rela-

tionship yet — and I'm not sure he wants it, either — I still feel uncomfortable keeping things from him. On the other hand, why tell him about a date with Gus, or having drinks with Bart in Vancouver, or anything else that could get magnified at this great distance? He has no reason to think I'm restricting my socializing to the women at the conference.

As I answer the knock on the door of my room, I realize I'm now calling this a date and not just a dinner out together, so I guess it is one. I wonder if Gus thinks the same.

We never get the chance to find out, because as we're about to hail a cab outside the hotel, Kevin pulls up in a taxi of his own.

"Ruby — where are you going?" he says from the backseat.

He won't let me explain that we're headed out for dinner together.

"No, no, don't go. I have too much to tell you."

Gus and I look at each other. As much as we want to grab our own cab, we're both sufficiently curious to hear what Kevin has to say.

We get into the cab with him, which surprises him as much as us.

"Come to dinner with us, then," I say. "We're not wasting our time in Banff eating at the hotel. You can leave us after dinner, okay?"

"But Bitsy's supposed to meet me later, Ruby. At least let me get out of the cab to go find her."

"Nothing doing," I say, "it's now or never."

"You can have a drink while we're eating," Gus says. "Unless you want to talk to us late tonight instead."

"You seem to be in a hurry to talk," I say to Kevin. Then I'm suddenly sorry for hassling him when he's no doubt had a rough time of it at the morgue.

"Sorry," I tell him. "You must be in bad shape from earlier."

"Yeah," he says, "let's just go." He eases back into his seat.

We direct the taxi to a Chinese place we've been told about, and we all go upstairs to the seating area for drinks and dinner.

"It was André," Kevin blurts out as soon as we're shown to our table with a view of the mountains. "I think I need a scotch.

"His face was pretty messed up, but I had no trouble recognizing him," he continues. "It made me sick, so they didn't keep me in the room long. This is the first time I've ever

296

had to do that as clergy — I still don't know why they chose me. Everyone here knew him as well as I did."

"Maybe they want to keep it quiet," Gus says, "and they didn't think you'd spread it around."

Oh, yeah, they really have the right person for secrecy. I don't think it matters, though — things like this have a tendency to get out one way or another.

"They questioned me for a while after I left the room and had some water," Kevin says.

"What did they ask you?" I say.

"How I thought it happened, which of course I had no idea about. I told them they were talking to the wrong person — that you were the one who saw the body, and that you also thought of smuggling André's backpack off the train so no one would take it by accident."

"*Smuggling?*" I say. "Could you have thought of a word that's any more incriminating? They probably think I pushed him overboard myself."

Gus smiles. "Don't worry about it, Ruby — I'll vouch for you. Although now that I think of it, maybe we were lucky that we hopped into the rabbi's cab before the police were at your door. I'll bet you're in for an interrogation later tonight when they find you."

He's right, and I'm not looking forward to it. Unfortunately, my conversation with Paul didn't make me feel any more ready for confrontations with the police, either. Paul's a lot more paranoid about this situation than I am. Maybe I can just refer them to him.

"You must have seen André's body right after he fell from the train," Kevin says.

"He had to have jumped from the very front cars," I say, "or have been thrown or whatever. When I saw him from the last car a minute or so later, he was facedown by the river bend. My guess is that if he took a leap from the train, he waited until it had just emerged from one of the Spiral Tunnels — otherwise, he would have been in total blackness."

"And if someone pushed him," Gus says, "they waited, too, until that instant when daylight flashed through the windows again. It's always a disorienting moment."

"This was carefully planned," I say, "no matter who caused it."

The three of us are gradually realizing that the alcohol is the only thing on our table that's disappearing. Kevin's had two scotches, and Gus and I are three-quarters through our bottle of wine, but none of us has touched the food.

"Do you want this boxed up?" the waiter finally asks, and we all shake our heads no.

"What a waste," I say, and the others look at me, not sure whether I'm talking about the food or the meaningless death we just witnessed today.

I guess I mean both.

40

Today our Temple Rita bus is taking a short sightseeing trip to Lake Louise, thirty minutes or so from Banff. I've always wanted to visit this place, and I'm glad I didn't heed Paul's advice to hop the next plane home. Although I feel as bad as everyone else about André's death, I can't say that my emotional ties are any stronger than those of the other congregants here. Besides, the police are assuming that we'll be in the area for the remainder of the ChoirFest if they need us — although, so far, they haven't contacted me specifically. I hear that their questioning has been quite methodical, and I have no doubt they'll get around to me soon.

Last night, of course, with the news so fresh, was a bummer from beginning to end. By the time Gus and I worked our way through the Chinese dinner that wasn't, we were no more in the mood to enjoy the evening than Kevin was. So much for the date I was keeping from Paul. Kevin didn't leave us early, and instead, we all took the same taxi back to the hotel. I fell into bed, no doubt helped along by the three glasses of wine, and didn't even hear Essie Sue when she unlocked the door to our room. I did hear the TV she turned on later, but I was so out of it that it was easy to ignore the noise. No way would I have been ready for a discussion with her about the events of the day, not that she didn't try to rouse me several times.

The windows of our bus are open, and the mountain air is beyond invigorating — it's making me feel alive again after a groggy morning. Even the thermos of coffee the hotel made for me is perfect, and helps to mute the incessant chatter all around me. I can't stand a lot of noise before about eleven o'clock — my ears just won't take it. I don't even like the radio in the morning, and I'm certainly not ready to interact with our group just now.

Lake Louise, a mile high in the Rockies near the Continental Divide, is filled with exquisite emerald green water. The guide tells us that the glaciers above Lake Louise grind the minerals from the streams into the lake waters, and that the sunlight reflected off the mineral sediment is what makes the water color so vivid. The lake is encircled by mountains, and later today we're taking a sightseeing lift halfway up the Lake Louise ski area, so we can look down at the lake and the peaks surrounding it. I can't wait.

First, though, we're invited to get off the bus and walk Lakeshore Trail, which follows the north shore to the far border of the lake. You don't even need to be a hiker to enjoy this walk — it's a stroll, really, through a wooded area by the water.

Lake Louise is an international tourist attraction, and like the Grand Canyon, it's easy to pick up several languages coming from those marveling at the views. I see a Scandinavian group ambling in front of me, and following them presents me with a perfect opportunity to ensure a few more minutes of solitude, where I'm not in reach of Essie Sue and company.

It's easy to daydream while I'm walking along, and I'm mesmerized by the few small boats bobbing in the water — I'd love to know where I could rent one. I can't stop the visions of both Paul and Gus running through my mind, although I'd rather imagine myself floating on that gentle green expanse out there. Who knows how cold it is, though — we *are* in Canada, after all, not like Barton Springs in Austin, where the water temperature is in the midsixties winter and summer.

I stay a few paces behind the group, happily detached from the chatter in what sounds like Swedish. I'm amazed at how tiny the lake is — like a jewel. When I first saw the "Mona Lisa" in person, I was surprised at how small that was, too — in both cases, celebrity seems to magnify reality.

My eyes can't focus on the faces of the group in front of me except for an occasional profile when one turns to another in conversation. That's why I'm surprised when I glimpse a face that seems familiar, looking back at me from those walking farthest ahead. Again, a hat shadowing the face — this time a brown, broad-brimmed Alpine mountaineer's fedora. I think it's a man, but it could be a woman, too — the figure is wearing khaki pants, a zippered jacket, and hiking boots. Whatever hair there is must be tucked under the hat and not visible. Not much *is* visible, since the group so far ahead of us is setting the pace for everyone else, and they're moving fast.

I hurry to catch up with them, weaving easily in and out of the crowd, since aside from the familiar figure, no one is paying the least bit of attention to me. I'm contrasting this with our own group from Eternal, where a stranger couldn't be a part of the crowd for thirty seconds without someone asking who, what, and why, and then reporting back to everyone else.

It's annoying not to be able to place the person who looked back at me, but it's obvious that this is the same face I saw for an instant on the train. This is a good time to satisfy my curiosity — I'm not meeting the others for a half hour. I've promised Kevin I'll go on the lift with him up the mountain, and in return, he's promised to pick up fresh batteries for my digital camera.

I'm jogging by the time I work my way to the front of the crowd — these people are making good time. First, I try to find the person on my own, but everyone looks alike. Most have on baseball caps or wool ski hats with parkas — there's not anything you could call a real hat in the bunch. Maybe I was hallucinating about the hat, so I examine the faces around me. Not a familiar puss in the lot.

When I don't see what I'm looking for, I interrupt a couple of conversations around me with questions in English that are obviously routinely understood, but which produce no good answers. A woman does remember briefly seeing someone with that hat, so I'm not crazy, but she shrugs when I ask which direction. So I guess this is another dead end, unless I stop in my tracks, turn around to face the upcoming hikers, and scrutinize the crowd.

Even this doesn't help, so I have no choice but to keep walking against the current of the crowd and back toward my starting point.

The lift isn't far from the lake, and Kevin's already there and pacing when I arrive.

"Look, Ruby, I made a mistake," he says. "I couldn't find the backup batteries you wanted, but I'm also not going up with you. I'll stay here at the bottom, where it's safe."

"Safe?" I say. "All this is safe, Kevin. They've put thousands of tourists on these chairlifts, and I've never heard of one falling off yet. It's supposed to be gorgeous up there at Whitehorn Lodge. Why miss it?"

"Okay, but only if you'll take one of the enclosed chairs."

I hadn't noticed, but Kevin's obviously already checked out the lifts and learned that there are two kinds — the open chairs that look like double garden swings, and the boxes with shaded plastic windows. Those hold four people, not two. But they're shielded from the wind and, in my opinion, from the best views. For anyone with a fear of heights, though, the box is the way to go.

"That's fine," I say. "I can always take the other kind after you and I make the ride if I want to try the open route."

We wait for the attendant to tell us when to jump onto the enclosed box as the mechanical pulley brings it around to where we're standing.

"It's rocking," Kevin says, and I have to give him a gentle push to get him inside before the lift continues up the mountainside without us.

"I'm right behind you," I say, and he slides into a seat. No one else has joined us, which is probably a good thing for Kevin, who's sitting stiffly at the edge of his chair.

"Relax and enjoy it," I say. "Look, you can almost reach out and touch the treetops. I'll bet that you can actually touch them in one of the open cars."

I can tell that the air's thinner as we ascend, and as advertised, the view is spectacular. Kevin's enjoying it in spite of himself.

"I'm glad I came," he says. "The lake looks like a postage stamp down there."

"You deserve some fun," I say. "Yesterday was rough."

"I guess I'll have to do the funeral," he says. "I've only done one suicide, and it was awful."

I hadn't even thought that far ahead, but he's probably right that the funeral will be in Eternal. I'm wondering how long they'll hold André's body here before his wife can claim it.

"Let's don't talk about it right now," I suggest. "We're about to jump off at the exit gate, so get ready."

Our getaway is perfectly satisfactory, except for the fact that once we hop out, we're met by Essie Sue and her cousin Belle.

"Let's have tea and low-fat muffins," Essie Sue says, "and we can talk about poor André."

"I'll pass," I say. "I was just telling Kevin that I want to save that conversation for down below."

"I don't want to talk, either," Kevin says.

"Well, can I at least tell you what gossip I've heard?" Essie Sue says.

"Can we stop you?" I say.

"The police took André's luggage this morning, and I heard they found some clues to his death," she says.

"They didn't take it while I was in the room," Kevin says. "It must have been later, after I'd gone. I wonder if they looked through my duffel, too. Some of my socks have holes in them."

"I'm sure they're not interested in your hole-y clothes," Belle says. "*Holy* clothes — get it?"

When her joke gets the reception it deserves, Belle loses interest, but Essie Sue's not deterred.

"Rabbi, I want you, in your clerical role, to see what other information you can dig up. No one was able to tell me exactly what those clues were."

"No thanks," Kevin says. "I've had all the talks with the police I want to have — I already told Ruby about it."

"And thanks to you, Ruby, I know next to nothing," Essie Sue says. "You were asleep last night when I came in, and sleeping when I got up this morning. What good are you as a roommate? I envisioned us as having a much better time than this."

Well, I didn't, but thanks to my artful dodging, I've managed to hold the damage to a minimum, and I'm pretty proud of myself. This rooming situation could have been a lot worse, although as I'm well aware, it's not over yet.

41

We end up having tea and muffins with Essie Sue and Belle after all, but I quickly realize that, as Essie Sue said, she really knows nothing more about the police investigation. One sure way to get rid of these two is to suggest a long walk — they're not big hikers — so I push Kevin to go with me.

"I'm not really a great walker, either, Ruby," he says to me. This is not exactly news, but I give him time to absorb the fact that if he turns me down, he's stuck with Essie Sue and Belle.

"Well, okay, I guess," he says. "Can we stop a lot?"

"Sure, Kevin," I say as soon as we're alone. "I just wanted an excuse to get away, and I'm more interested in taking photos than racking up the miles."

I wouldn't miss this photo op for the world — the vista before us is spectacular, and the light today is shimmering and perfect. The lake looks almost lost among the snow-capped peaks, but my lens has no problem picking up that luminescent green.

Kevin's patient as I take advantage of the good light, and at lunchtime we slip away to a café that's adjacent to the larger restaurant, where I'm sure Essie Sue will be holding court.

"I could stay up here all day," I say when we're finished with lunch, "but I'm antsy about that police interrogation. I'm also curious to hear people's reactions now that the news is public. I'm wondering if some of them will be going home early — Irene, for instance; she was close to André, and maybe she'll want to be with his wife."

"How about Dr. Goldman?" Kevin says. "The whole quartet was tight."

"It's possible. Kevin, would you be disappointed if we went down the mountain now instead of waiting for the others?"

"Are you kidding?" he says. "I'm ready for a nap — yesterday did me in."

"Good. It'll give me time to poke around the lobby and see what's going on."

It's early afternoon, and the tourists are swarming all over the place. I thought the lifts might be less busy now, but people are hopping on and off as fast as the cars can handle them. I see a few enclosed cabins, but most of the lifts are open ones.

"Let's do it, Kevin," I say. "Who knows when we'll ever be back here?"

"You're not suggesting we take one of the open lifts?"

"We can link arms," I say. "Once you're on there, you're going to love it. The view out the plastic windows of the other car doesn't compare with these. And they're much more frequent."

"I don't know, Ruby. Maybe. I'll think about it."

"Fair enough," I say. "I don't want to push you, and we can go separately if you want. But you're going to have to make a fast decision once we're on the launching platform. If you don't jump, you miss it and it goes on by."

The lifts are moving quickly, so although we're waiting in a glut of humanity, the process of getting all those people down the mountain is quite efficient.

"If you do it," I say while we're standing there, "I want to get a snapshot of you once you've jumped aboard. You'll never believe you did it once you get home."

"It'll be proof," he says. "But that's not your camera in your hand — what is that thing?"

"My camera's out of juice," I say. "I used

311

up the battery taking all those photos of the views. This is my PDA — personal digital assistant. It has a camera, voice recorder, extra memory, and everything else I could cram into it. It's like a backup."

"Whatever."

We're standing side by side, and Kevin straightens his shoulders. I think he's getting up the nerve to do it. I take his hand.

"Are we set for this, then?" I say.

"Yep," he says, tightening his grip.

When the lift finally glides right in front of us, I go first. Then so many things happen at once that my brain can't put them in sequence.

For openers, Kevin lets go of my hand, and I figure he must feel more secure grabbing the pole attached to the lift. At the same time, I hear an odd little nervous hum that seems vaguely familiar. I leap on board and turn around to aim my camera in Kevin's direction, so I can get a photo of him jumping on.

The weight of his body shakes the floor of the lift, but I can still get a shot if I hurry. The lift keeps moving and leaves the platform behind us. I look in the viewfinder and take my picture just in time. There's only one problem. The person I see through the

camera lens isn't Kevin.
  It's Rose.

42

I'm absolutely sure I'm hallucinating. I already know my good friend Rose Baker didn't make the trip to Canada — she stayed home in Eternal because she'd traveled to Ohio earlier this year to see Serena's sister. Rose didn't want to leave her family again so soon, so she passed up the choir trip.

I give my head a shake to straighten out my brain, and flop down on the hard bench. This makes the car lurch, and this woman who can't be Rose suddenly lands on the seat beside me.

"Where's Kevin?" I say. "Did he lose his nerve?" A stupid remark, but I'm not following this at all.

The passenger just stares at me, humming that odd little tune that comes out of Rose when she's stressed.

"Rose?" I say.

Fedora and all, it's Rose — there's no

mistaking her face now, but I needed to hear the hum again to put it all together.

As if to assure me, she takes her hat off and throws it down at our feet.

"Don't tell me you weren't expecting me," she says.

"I'm dumbfounded," I say, and then I figure it out and have to smile. "Wait a minute — did you and Kevin get together on this? He stepped back and let you on here as a surprise? I didn't even think he could keep a secret, frankly. Did you decide to fly up at the last minute?"

"I've been here awhile," she says, "as you well know." She's not smiling back.

"Look," I say, "I don't know anything. I need a minute to work this out — I'm totally confused. That was you on the train? And by the lake?"

"You saw me on the train before it even happened," she says. "And then after, by the lake."

"I saw someone familiar," I say, "but certainly not you. I never remotely believed it was you — why would I? So why the elaborate hide-and-seek, babe? You wasted two days when we could have hung out together — I certainly could have used you with all that was going on. Do you know about what's happened?"

"You're saying you didn't recognize me?" she says.

"Not until now."

Rose visibly slumps in her seat.

"I don't believe it," she says. "You know, Ruby, you wouldn't be a part of this at all if you hadn't caught sight of me on the train. I'd been so good at staying away from all of you. Why did you have to be in that part of the train when the entire Temple Rita choir had seats somewhere else?"

I'm getting frustrated now, and my voice shows it. "What in the world are you talking about, Rose? Quit playing around."

"You're right," she says, moving closer to me. "I have very little time to do what I have to do. This is only a fifteen-minute ride, and we've thrown away five already. I've timed this lift twice, and we'll be passing over the ravine in another five."

She's coming close, almost as if to give me an affectionate hug despite her demeanor. But instead of sensing her arm circling my waist, I feel a prickly jab in my ribs, like a pinprick through my sweater, only a bit sharper.

"Ouch," I say, moving over, "your bracelet or something's sticking me. Rose, are you upset about André — is that why you're so agitated? You did hear he was —"

"Killed. Yes, obviously I know. You saw me only a short while before I killed him."

I feel myself slipping into some alternate universe — this is too much to absorb at one time. Not only don't I believe I'm hearing what I just heard, but I'm pretty sure I'm losing my senses. I'd chalk it all up to some sort of mental breakdown if I wasn't suddenly much more concerned with the sharp pain in my side.

"Yes, it's a bone-handled knife I bought at a gift shop in Banff," Rose says. "And you do know I grew up with knives. You learn a lot when your father's a lox cutter in a New York deli. He taught me a lot about biology, too — I know exactly where the heart lies under the ribs."

Her grip is firm, and I don't think I can safely move, or yell, either — not that anyone would hear me; the lifts aren't that close together, and it's windy up here. But my head is clear now — danger can do that. I stop trying to understand it all, and focus on the more immediate peril. I need to distract her.

"Why do you need to kill me, too?" I say.

"I told you," she says. "If you hadn't seen me, I would have flown home from Banff right away, and I'd be back in Eternal by now, paying a condolence call on Sara. But

I couldn't take that chance. When I saw you speak to the conductor, and caught sight of the police at the train station, I knew you had recognized me. I kept tabs on you at the lake, and followed you up the mountain."

"But I didn't recognize you," I say. "I had no idea who that was."

"I couldn't take the risk," she says. "The connection could have come to you at any time, even if you hadn't put it all together yet."

"You're here, and I still haven't put it all together," I say, moving slightly away from her. "Not you."

"Whoa," she says, and I feel the point of the knife again.

Rose manages to take quick glimpses of the mountainside as we go down. I don't want to remember that she's looking for the ravine she talked about.

I need to keep her talking. "Why did you do it?" I ask. "And why here?"

"The gossip in Eternal," she says. "I heard they'd discovered Serena's poisoning, and Joellyn confirmed it, so I had to see André right away. I wanted him to know I'd done it for us — I'd been hoping he'd never find out she didn't die of a heart attack."

"You and André? I thought Serena and

318

André . . ."

"It was all her, not him — she took him from me. I discovered a letter from him in Serena's car one day when we were riding somewhere. I didn't tell either of them that I had it. Once I got rid of her, though, I knew he'd come back to me. And when it was known Serena had been murdered, he'd be a prime suspect — he used to give her B_{12} shots, for God's sake. I thought we could stay in Canada, or abroad, and be safe. But when I told him why we should run away, he said he was horrified. Repelled. I took all the risks, and he's repelled? He's going to turn me in? No way."

My head might be clear now, but more like frozen clear. I'm still feeling paralyzed — the knife's too close to take chances.

"What do you want?" I finally say.

"Easy. You're going to jump when we're over the ravine, or be killed instantly now. I'm good at this, Ruby — make no mistake. I've killed two people — a third won't make any difference at all."

"There'll be questions — you won't get away with it. Kevin must have seen you, too."

"I doubt it — he hesitated and moved away, decided not to jump on here with you. I merely stepped in front of him — he only saw my back. Besides, I have two chances. If I get away unnoticed when the lift reaches the bottom of the mountain, that'll be the best I can hope for, and I'll head for the airport. If someone down there does stop me, I'll deal with it. No one suspects me of anything. I'll be as shocked over your terrible accidental fall as everyone else."

"Your husband and daughter will know you left Eternal," I say. "Are you going to trust Ray and Jackie not to tell, when even André wouldn't go along with you?"

"I've taken care of that," Rose says. "I was depressed over my father's death two years ago and then Serena's, and Ray agreed to have me go away for treatment in Ohio. Discreetly and quietly. If I'm recognized, and I won't be, then I left the treatment facility to join the choir here. A messier explanation, but what evidence would they have that I made you fall? Besides, it's not going to happen."

"But maybe —"

"Shut up, Ruby — it's not important to you. Nothing will be."

She's right about that — I'd better deal with priorities first, since it's obvious I'm not going to talk her out of this. She's planned her nasty surprise too well. My only hope is to wrestle the knife away from her right now or to jump before I'm directly over the ravine.

And if I do come away from this alive, I have a surprise of my own for Rose.

43

Rose Baker may have been my friend for years, but I've never had to size her up as if she were a middleweight coming at me in the ring — never mind one who hits below the belt. I'd say we weigh the same, but she has about four inches on me. My core body strength probably beats hers, which would mean more if she wasn't already holding a knife so close to my pounding heart.

Her arms are much longer than mine, too — I know that because of the way she's able to wrap one of them around me from behind while keeping her weapon steady with the other.

"Don't even think about it, Ruby," she says, as if reading my mind. "You can't begin to grab hold of me while I've got this blade pointing through your clothes — I can stick you before you'd have the op-portunity to wrest away. You'll have a better chance of jumping clean than wounded."

She's offering me a good reason for leaping down into a ravine? Give me a break, Rose. You just want to make absolutely sure that I'm not found with a knife wound — it wouldn't look good on the accident report. But the choice she's presenting represents a certain weakness on her part — I'm thinking she'll do a lot to keep from stabbing me as I fall over the rail between me and oblivion.

One thing's certain — I have seconds to make my move. We're passing over a thick stand of tall cedars, not my idea of a safe fall, but better than the wide-open vista ahead of us. If I thought I could take her, I would, but I don't think I have the leverage to throw her off the lift without having that knife go into me first. And I just don't relish the idea of a wrestling match all the way down — I think I'd come out the loser. A fanatical killer is an opponent I totally respect.

She has the knife in her right hand, so I push her left hand away as hard as I can, twisting her body away from me while I unlatch the rail holding me in. But the movement also coils her right arm closer around me, and I feel the point of the blade ripping into my stomach — her aim has slipped a few inches in the melee. Reflexively, I push the knife away as I jump, and I'm pretty sure it goes into some part of her — not that I can afford to worry about that right now.

I'm counting on my two arms to hang on to one of those very tall cedar trees, but I can't calculate how flimsy a treetop can be when a human body comes whirling into it. The trees are growing out of the side of the mountain very close to me, but I have no idea what the fall will be like if I miss. The surface slamming up to meet me will be a slanting one, and might only intensify the impact of my plunge.

Even though the wind has died down as we've descended, the slender treetop bends with me on it, and I can't stay on, even with both my legs wrapped around the branches. I feel myself falling to the ground — a crooked or straight landing, I don't know. But the tree has broken my dive, at least, and a part of my pant leg is hooked on one of the thick lower branches.

I'm down, I'm relatively alive, and I'm conscious enough to scream for the time it takes for the next open lift to pass by.

44

I awake with Essie Sue peering over my bed, so I know I'm not dreaming — this is not the person I'd waste a drug-induced hallucination on.

"You're in a hospital in Banff," she says, "and you're not supposed to be disturbed."

"So why are you disturbing me?" I ask, and immediately regret it because even moving my lips makes my head ache.

I whisper, which isn't as painful, so she leans farther over me. "How badly am I hurt?" I say.

"Not much," she says. "Only a broken ankle and a stab wound."

Oh, good. I'd like to know what her definition of *much* is. I close my eyes and decide to get my bad news from someone less anxious to deliver it.

I can feel the buzzer that's been wrapped loosely around my left wrist, so I press it for the nurse.

"Can I see a doctor?" I whisper when an orderly arrives. "And may I please have some privacy for a few minutes?"

"Go away," Essie Sue tells the orderly, "this woman needs her privacy to recuperate."

I point as well as I can manage at Essie Sue, and fortunately, the orderly gets it.

"But I'm her caretaker," I hear Essie Sue say, and I shake my head as vigorously as possible without taking the top of my skull off.

"You'll have to come back later," the man says to her.

"Her clergyman's here," Essie Sue says, apparently hoping to hear secondhand what she can't witness for herself. On her way out the door she gestures to Kevin.

"It's okay," I say. "He can come in."

"Ruby, I feel awful," he says. "Can you make me feel any better about this?"

This is what I most love about Kevin and Essie Sue — they're never self-absorbed.

"Don't expect too much of me," I say. "I'm learning I have a few problems of my own. Can we deal with yours later?"

"But if I hadn't finked out, you wouldn't be in the hospital. I lost my nerve about jumping on that open lift, and before I knew it, someone had taken my place. The police

326

told us later that it was Rose Baker, of all people."

"They found her? How long have I been here?" I ask.

"All afternoon. It's past dinnertime now. Rose collapsed after the sightseeing lift came down from the mountain by Lake Louise. She got off and was trying to walk away when she passed out in a pool of blood."

"Where is she? Do they know she tried to kill me? And that she killed André and Serena?"

"Huh? How do you know that? I'm not sure what they've discovered. They found you right after she came down the mountain, and I know they took her in an ambulance — to this hospital, I think. And it's all my fault."

"Why were the police even involved with her?" I say.

"Because when they picked you up, you kept yelling that Rose had pushed you off the lift and knifed you. I guess someone in authority put it all together. The knife had come down with you — caught in your clothes, I think."

"I'm glad, at least, that she didn't get rid of it herself," I say. "But we need to post a guard outside this room. Can you take care of that? I'm scared she'll come in here to finish the job — she was possessed."

"I'll tell Essie Sue to do it," he says. "I'm too upset."

"No Essie Sue," I say. "Look, Kevin, do me just one favor. Do you know where my cell phone is?"

"I don't know where your stuff is — maybe it's lost. You can have my cell, but it's not set for international calls."

"Don't worry about it," I say. "They'll just charge you extra if I can get to an operator. I'll pay you back."

I grab his cell and make sure he stays to give the operator his identification — then I ask him to leave and stand by the door, just in case.

Thank heavens I find Paul at work.

"Ruby, what happened? I just heard you were in surgery, and I was trying to get in touch with the doctors. I'm coming up there."

"I'm okay," I say. "But, Paul, I need you to help now, and if you're flying here, you'll be out of reach. I'm worried that the doctors will give me something that'll knock me out, or that they'll take my phone away. You've got to stand in for me."

I persuade him to stay there and help me by phone or fax or whatever, and I try to remember the whole sequence of events this afternoon — everything Rose said and did. I'm petrified she could get away with this.

"How are you going to do it all?" I say. "And what are you going to do first?"

"Calm down, honey," he says. "I do this for a living. I'm calling the police to get a guard for your room from hospital security, and I'll check on Rose's condition. Then I'll do everything else."

"But I don't even know where my clothes are," I say. "They must have cut them off of me. I have to get my cell phone — I hid it in my jacket pocket."

"That's the least of your worries," he says. "I'll call your hospital room."

"First, they might not let me take calls," I say. "But that's not the problem. I need the cell for other reasons."

"Later, Ruby. Let me get started."

"No, Paul, you have to know this. My phone has a camera and a voice recorder. Since I was set up to photograph Kevin as he jumped onto the lift, I got a shot of Rose instead, and I recorded everything she said."

45

"People have flown home with worse injuries than a broken ankle," I tell my partner Milt Aboud as he passes a warm poppy-seed bagel across the quilt where I'm propped up on my favorite down pillows. Oy Vey and Chutzpah want to share the cream cheese with me, but nothing doing — they'll have to be satisfied with being the center of attention at this impromptu brunch taking place on the queen-size bed in my house on Watermelon Lane.

Milt has brewed a strong Italian roast to make sure I overcome my painkillers enough to describe every detail of what is undoubtedly the hottest topic ever to make the rounds in Eternal, Texas. This occasion was supposed to be coffee and bagels with just me and Milt, but when he left The Hot Bagel to come over here, Essie Sue and Kevin somehow got the word, picked up Bitsy, and joined us.

"I still think you came home too early, Ruby," Essie Sue says. "It's just like you to defy your doctor's advice. And after I offered to nurse you back to health, too. If I'd had the chance, I would have asked them to do a little liposuction while they were sewing up your stomach wound."

Milt snorts — he still hasn't learned to hold it in when he's around Essie Sue. "So that's why you left the hospital so soon," he says to me, "to ditch the personalized nursing care."

"I wanted my own cozy bed," I say, "before Essie Sue's care turned into coronary care. And I was uneasy with Rose being just down the hall, even if she was unconscious for a while. I answered every question the authorities could throw at me, and by then I was itching to get out of there."

"I heard when she woke up she accused *you* of attacking *her* with the knife," Kevin says.

"She did," I say, "but that didn't hold up when the gift shop clerk in Banff identified her as the person who bought a souvenir knife from them the day before she used it on me. And after she heard her words recorded on my organizer, she opted for a deal."

"You were going to take my picture when

I jumped on board, weren't you?" Kevin says. "I remember talking to you about using your electronic organizer as a backup camera."

"Yep, and it's a voice recorder, also. I had it turned on along with the camera, and I left it that way. Rose was so intent on taking me by surprise and hiding her knife under her sleeve that I doubt she even noticed the camera when she jumped on — I was so shocked that I almost dropped it myself. We had other things to think about, and I just let it fall into my big jacket pocket. I thought about it midway, though, when she was telling me about killing André and Serena."

"Rose, a killer?" Essie Sue repeats for the umpteenth time. "Never in a million years would I have suspected. I'm speechless."

Not quite, but close — this is the first time I've seen her willing to take a backseat in any conversation.

"What did these women see in that guy André?" Bitsy says. "He gave me the creeps, and he wasn't even sexy."

I never imagined Bitsy and I would have anything in common, but I must admit she's echoing my thoughts exactly. Not that it's very charitable of her to be knocking one of the victims. André Korman didn't kill Serena — his biggest crime was his cheatin' heart, I guess, along with the chutzpah and greed to think he could franchise Jewish philosophy.

"It's Rose who has me bewildered, too — she was my friend," I tell Milt, trying to pretend the others aren't hovering. "We've only been home from Canada for two days, and everyone seems to think I have more information here than I had in Banff. The truth is that the whole Canadian experience now seems fuzzy to me — I think I'm still in shock from the afternoon on the lift. Paul says he's protecting me from information overload, but he should know better. The police haven't even told me about Rose's status in Canada, since she killed one victim there and the other here in Eternal.

"What have you all learned?" I ask. My pain might have prevented me from being my terrier-doggish self, but I doubt Essie Sue's been as passive. She'd be surprised to know I'm hoping to discover as much from her as she is from me.

"I've found out some of the gossip from this end," she says, brushing away little Chutzpah, who responds by digging his claws into her cashmere cardigan. He's not so easy to get rid of, though she doesn't know it yet. I try to retrieve him before he tears any threads — he doesn't know who he's dealing with, either.

"So give," I tell Essie Sue by way of diversion, "who did you talk to?"

"That's a secret," she says, "but suffice it to say that Rose was a busy little bee. I have it on good authority from a hairdresser who shall remain anonymous that she had an affair with André right under his wife's nose before he fell in love with Serena Salit."

"In love?" Bitsy says. "Maybe in lust."

"In lust with Rose, maybe," Essie Sue says, "but he definitely fell for Serena emotionally as well as physically. Apparently, Rose couldn't take it and decided to get rid of her rival. She put a fast-acting poison in the same type of syringe André had been using to give B_{12} shots to some of the choir members, including Serena. He gave them all the time to his health food store customers. Since Serena was always nervous when she had to solo, Rose suggested to her that day at the temple latke party that she have André give her a shot just for a boost."

"It's not a tranquilizer," Milt says.

"No, but people were always convinced the shots made them feel good," Essie Sue says, "and André was glad to oblige. I heard the poison might have been nicotine sulfate — it works within minutes and stops heart action. That's just gossip, though."

"As if gossip would stop you," Milt says. "But it is amazing that André gave Serena the shot that killed her."

"Yes," Essie Sue says, ignoring his little dig. "And when Rose confronted André on the train that day with how she'd set him up, she expected him to take her back — especially with the threat of exposure hanging over his head. The police would never believe he hadn't known he was injecting poison — and no one would have suspected Rose."

"I gather from what Rose told me," I say, "that André was more of a mensch —"

"That means a real man," Essie Sue tells Milt, who answers that he already knew.

"— more of a mensch than Rose thought he'd be," I continue. "He told Rose he was horrified at what she had done, and that he had not only loved Serena, but was hoping to leave his wife for her.

"Rose thought she had no choice but to get rid of André before he told the police. My guess is that she revealed herself to him when he was alone and coming out of the bathroom near the space between the engine and the next car, where he took all his photos — it was outside and away from the reflection from the windows. When he reacted badly, she knew she had to get rid of him fast. She was also able to take advantage of the fact that the train was in and out of those tunnels — passengers on the train were distracted by the alternate light and darkness. I doubt she planned that, but it helped. When I took pictures from the last car of the train, I saw the body that Rose had pushed from the forward car minutes before. It was André."

"And she left that syringe we found in his backpack," Kevin says.

"Plus the letter to Serena," I say. "She found it in Serena's car one day and kept it. Rose must have wanted to emphasize the connection between André and Serena for the police's benefit when he went missing, so she made sure it was in his backpack. Then, when André didn't show up or wasn't discovered, people would think he committed suicide or ran away."

"So do you think she told André and prepared for a possible rejection at the same time?" Milt says.

"There's no doubt she was cunning," I say. "I think she truly believed André would have no choice but to go away with her, but she knew what she'd do if he didn't. She planned everything."

46

Email to: Ruby
From: Nan
Subject: RE: The latest about Rose

I'm still reeling from the news — don't forget, babe, I want every detail as you hear it. Thanks for the calls and email updates.

I'll bet Rose couldn't wait to go to Ohio when she heard that Serena's sister, Joellyn, had the laptop — and, of course, the information on it only confirmed what Rose already knew about the affair. Plus, the exposure of Serena's fears about André's little Kabbalah cult helped create other possible reasons for her murder — Rose must have been thrilled at those discoveries. Did Rose trick Joellyn

into helping arrange for her alibi, too
— Rose's supposed treatment at the
mental health facility in Ohio? That
was a great cover story for her flight
to Canada.

Email to: Nan
From: Ruby
Subject: Answers

Yeah, Joellyn was more than happy
to help arrange the stay at the clinic
for Rose; she didn't suspect a thing
— not that any of us did. Rose never
showed up, of course, and flew to
Canada instead. Since she'd told
Joellyn she wouldn't hear from her
for a while, the plan went perfectly.
Joellyn kept the visit to the mental
health clinic a secret — it was logical
that Rose wouldn't have wanted her
friends in Eternal to know about her
problems.

The authorities aren't sure yet how
she obtained the poison, although at
one time she had access to Serena's

keys, and there was always a key to Dr. Bart's clinic on them. Rose's husband, Ray, is a printer, too, anduses many chemicals. It's possible she knew a supplier through him. The police have probably found out plenty during questioning that they haven't released yet.

It also makes sense to me now why Rose avoided me for so long after her visit to Ohio — she knew I'd ask a lot of questions.

Changing the subject — which I'm desperately trying to do around here so I can recover faster — I'm forwarding you a cheery email Gus wrote. He says he misses me. He also sent me some flowers — nice, huh?

Email to: Ruby
From: Nan
Subject: Avoidance

Gus's email was indeed *nice*, but what's up with he who has no name?

Has Paul fallen into a well or some-thing? You haven't mentioned him since you returned home, and I cer-tainly hope you're not expecting me to forget he exists.

Email to: Nan
From: Ruby
Subject: When did you ever forget *anything?*

I *was* avoiding this subject, because it's like cotton candy — I can't bite into it without having it evaporate. Paul learned from reading the Cana-dian police reports that Gus was with me when I told the conductor about seeing the body, and that we'd spent time together during the trip. You know how jealous he was over Ed Levinger, and I simply didn't want another scene over someone I'd just met, so I hadn't mentioned it.

Bottom line is that we're in an awkward place right now. I want to remind him that we're not in an exclusive relationship, but whenever I bring it up, I feel I'm going to hurt him. So I keep quiet. He, on the other hand, doesn't really want to get into anything with me while I'm still recovering. We're both futzing around and feeling distant.

Email to: Ruby
From: Nan
Subject: I get it

I didn't mean to put you on the spot, but I'm glad I asked. Maybe you should follow the rabbi's lead and stir up a little trouble online. What I'm reading into this is that you honestly don't want to settle down just now. Am I right? If so, I'll respect that, and I'll quit hounding you about it. So do you want me to have Paul? Just kidding.

Email to: Nan
From: Ruby
Subject: Your query

Well, I wouldn't go that far. You might want to meet Gus sometime, though — he lives a lot closer to you.

Funny you should mention our rabbi and his online pursuits. I'll definitely send you updates on the latest. Kevin just called here in a panic — one of his virtual cuties just showed up on his doorstep!

RUBY'S CHANUKAH LATKES

6 large potatoes
1/2 small onion
2 eggs
1/4 cup Matzo meal
Salt and pepper

Serves 4 to 6

Peel and grate 6 large potatoes and half small onion. Soak mixture in water, then drain until dry. Add 2 eggs, one quarter cup Matzo meal, salt and pepper to taste.

Heat one cup oil and drop medium spoonfuls into hot oil for thin and crispy pancakes. Fry until brown and golden. From frying pan, place latkes on paper towels to absorb extra oil.

Serve with applesauce and sour cream. Enjoy!

ACKNOWLEDGMENTS

To Ruby's greatest cheering section — the family I love: David Weizenbaum, Suzanne Weizenbaum, Jon Weizenbaum and Nancy Nussbaum, Emma and Camille Weizenbaum.

To my friends Sue and Ned Bloomfield, Lindsy Van Gelder, Kathi Stein, Olga Wise, and the Shoal Creek Writers — Nancy Bell, Judith Austin Mills, Eileen Joyce, Dena Garcia, and Linda Foss — for their love and support.

My thanks to Helen Rees of the Helen Rees Agency, for her enthusiasm and down-to-earth advice, and to Sarah Knight, my editor at Scribner, for her invaluable contributions to the book.

My appreciation to Angella Baker, Meg Carstens, and Erica Gelbard of Scribner, Joan Mazmanian of the Helen Rees Agency, Charlene Crilley for Ruby's website, www.sharonkahn.com, and all those at Scribner who helped guide the book along its way.

My very special thanks to Susanne Kirk, dear friend and editor, whose belief in the Ruby series launched a new chapter in my life. I'll always be grateful for your constant help and encouragement.

ABOUT THE AUTHOR

Sharon Kahn has worked as an arbitrator, attorney, and freelance writer. She is a graduate of Vassar College and the University of Arizona Law School. The mother of three, and the former wife of a rabbi, she lives in Austin, Texas. *Fax Me a Bagel,* a Ruby, the Rabbi's Wife novel and her mystery debut, appeared in 1998 and was nominated for an Agatha Award. Visit her website at www.sharonkahn.com.

The employees of Thorndike Press hope you have enjoyed this Large Print book. All our Thorndike and Wheeler Large Print titles are designed for easy reading, and all our books are made to last. Other Thorndike Press Large Print books are available at your library, through selected bookstores, or directly from us.

For information about titles, please call:
  (800) 223-1244

or visit our Web site at:
  www.gale.com/thorndike
  www.gale.com/wheeler

To share your comments, please write:
  Publisher
  Thorndike Press
  295 Kennedy Memorial Drive
  Waterville, ME 04901